Despite Everything

Despite Everything

KAREN ROSSI

A Karen Rossi Romance

Wisteria Publications

Wisteria Publications
507-4 Briar Hill Heights
New Tecumseth, ON
L9R 1Z7

Despite Everything
ISBN: 978-1-988763-11-8

Published in Canada 2018

Layout and Cover Art by Taria van Weesenbeek

Please contact the author at brooks.kaarina@gmail.com for any questions or comments.

This book is a work of fiction. Names, characters and incidents are a product of the author's imagination or are used fictitiously.

Dedication

Dedicated to the memory of Alice Davey, an Ojibwa woman from Longlac Reserve 58, and the mother of my best friends, Sylvia and Bonnie Davey.

Other Books by Karen Rossi

"Portraits of Love" Series
    Dare to Dream
    Dare to Love
    Dare to Surrender
    Dare to Trust

Beyond Forgiveness
No Home for My Heart

Acknowledgements

I want to thank Taria van Weesenbeek who has given so generously of her time to bring this novel to life.

Chapter One

The bus had definitely seen better days. It now deposited Christina Lawrence, along with her small son, Christopher, and two large suitcases onto the side of the gravel road, and then continued on, leaving them both coughing in a cloud of dust and exhaust fumes. Probably that monstrosity of a vehicle had never been subjected to an exhaust test way up here in the middle of the Northern Ontario woods. For sure it would never pass the test in Southern Ontario, but Tina didn't voice her opinion aloud. Christopher might take it as a sign he'd been in some great danger while on the bus.

She brushed the road dust off her stylish spring jacket, while Christopher blew up his snubby freckled nose, like Winnie-the-Pooh blowing a feather. The scrawny, dusty spruce trees guarding each side of the gravel road didn't reveal what lay hidden in the forest, but Tina knew there was life somewhere behind them. Through the dirty bus windows she'd had the occasional glimpse of a fast-flowing river, a sparkling lake, or a small cabin.

"When is that guy coming to pick us up?" Christopher

asked and swatted at a black fly that was taking a bite off his arm. A red splotch appeared and he quickly wiped the blood off with his other hand. "Yuck!"

Tina cursed herself for not putting the bug spray into her purse. It was in one of the suitcases and she wasn't going to start digging through them here on the dusty roadside.

But she did have a small bottle of hand sanitizer, which she dug out of her purse. "Here, use this to wash off the blood," she told Christopher and squirted a small blob onto his thin arm.

"I hate that smell," the boy objected, but obediently rubbed the sanitizer onto his pale skin. "The black fly wasn't dirty."

"Never know where that fly might have been," Tina said. "You know how dirty houseflies are."

Christopher squinted at the leftovers of the tiny fly on his arm. "That wasn't a housefly," he observed.

"No, but still . . ." Tina knew she was being neurotic, but no wonder. She was totally out of her element here at Greenstone Reserve—wherever that village was hiding. And she had no idea what the next year would bring. Or maybe she would stay here only six months. How about three? And if that chief didn't appear soon to get them, she might just turn around and head back to Spruce Falls on the next bus.

If there was a return bus today. Maybe she and Christopher would end up standing here as the night fell and the mosquitoes ate the two of them alive.

Tina shuddered and waved one of the pests away from her face. Whose idea was this, anyway? Her own, of course. Most of her fellow graduates had secured teaching jobs in the Toronto area, but it had always been her plan to teach outside the city limits—prefer-ably as close as possible to the Arctic Circle. It was her stubborn streak of do-goodism that had set her off on this path. And—she reluctantly admitted—her desire for independence from her loving but overbearing par-ents. If she hadn't had Christopher, she would have gone to Africa or some other part of the Third World where teachers were hard to come by. But with a small son, she'd decided to stay in Canada. So here she was, waiting on this god-forsaken roadside somewhere close to—she hoped—the Greenstone Ojibwa Reserve.

That chief had better arrive soon or she would break down and cry. She swatted at a deer fly that had been buzzing around her head for the last five minutes and had finally settled on her hair. Well, she'd asked for this, and this was what she'd got. Kind of late to complain about it.

It was the way she'd always been since her early teens when she'd become aware of the poverty around the world. The realization that everyone didn't live in big houses like the ones in her own comfortable, upper-class neighbourhood, had been a real eye-opener. It had got her volunteering at food-banks and setting up toy-drives before Christmas. So it was only natural she would eventually find her way to some far-away place where, she hoped, she could have a posi-tive impact. Having worked in marketing for a few years after getting her MA, she had decided to go back to university to get her teaching degree and head off to wherever teachers were needed. Like here, in North-ern Ontario.

Christopher plunked himself down to sit on a suit-case. "I don't like these black flies!" he whimpered. His arms were now sporting several red bumps, plus white stripes where his finger nails had scraped the skin.

"Stop scratching, Christopher!" Tina said crossly. "You'll get an infection. Just rub them."

"Well, they itch," the boy whined, but obediently started to rub his palms up and down his arms. "When's he coming? I'm hungry."

"Soon, I'm sure."

But she was far from sure. By now twenty minutes had passed and not a living soul had appeared on the scene. She glanced at her watch—a beautiful diamond studded one, a graduation gift from her parents—and shook her head. It was past seven, so no wonder Christopher was hungry. The boy was having a growth spurt and was always looking for something to stuff into his mouth.

Tina groped in her large shoulder bag for something that might resemble food and came up with half a granola bar. The wrapping had slipped off and was crumpled up somewhere in the depths of the bag, along with crumbs of oats and raisins. Damn! Now she'd have to empty the whole thing out and clean it. Later.

She wiped the bar off with a tissue and handed it to her son. "Here, this'll hold you till Mr. Abraham comes. We'll get dinner at the reserve."

She hoped. Was the restaurant even open at this hour? She knew there was at least one diner because she'd looked at the facilities available on the reserve on the internet. There was also, she'd read, a Hudson's Bay store, a medical clinic with a doctor who visited intermittently, a church, a cemetery and a hotel with a bar. She'd reserved a room for herself and Christopher there for an indefinite period till they could find a house.

Okay, thinking about it now in the clear light of day, she knew she'd made a rather rash and hasty decision to come here, but when she'd seen the job posting, she'd decided to send in her application quickly before someone else stole the "ideal" job from under her. The letter of acceptance had come so quickly she'd begun to wonder if anyone else had even applied. And they'd hired her with no personal interview, just on the basis of her documents. It all sounded pretty suspicious. Applying for the job was probably a huge mistake on her part. At this moment it was beginning to seem so, anyway.

Tina brushed a deer fly off Christopher's golden blond hair. So like his father's and so unlike her own. Henry Nelson, the handsome intern who'd engaged with her in creating the boy, was now paying child support from his generous gynecological earnings.

She'd never been able to understand how a woman could get pregnant in this day and age with all the birth control methods available. But a woman obviously could. She didn't, for a second, rue the day her baby was born, but finding out she was pregnant had been a totally different story. Taking a screaming fit was a mild way of describing it. But she'd got through it all with the help of her parents. She'd gone back home and they had looked after Christopher since the day the baby was born.

"Nana said we shouldn't come here," Christopher now spoke up.

Actually, Christopher didn't speak anymore. He whined. He'd been whining since a few weeks before they left. And her mother had been sniffling just about as long. It had been downright annoying. It wasn't like they were moving to the moon or something. Big Thunder could be reached by air in a couple of hours from Toronto. And then there was a four-hour Greyhound ride to Spruce Falls along the Trans Canada Highway, plus a bumpy forty-minute ride from the main highway to this place in a dilapidated local vehicle, which maybe could loosely be called a bus.

And now they'd been waiting an undetermined number of minutes here on the roadside. Where the hell was Big Chief?

Tina looked with apprehension at the sun that was sinking too close to the tops of the spindly spruce trees. She'd done enough camping in the wilds of Algonquin Provincial Park to know the sunset would bring hoards of mosquitoes. And the insect repellent was handily tucked away in one of the suitcases. Which one? No idea. How stupid of her. It was the beginning of July, so she should have known black flies and mosquitoes, not to mention deerflies and any number of other biting, sucking insects would be around.

She shooed Christopher off the blue suitcase he was sitting on and flopped it onto its back. Mentally crossing her fingers she unzipped it. Let it be this one! But after pulling out most of Christopher's clothing— and piling them on top of the red suitcase, she gave up and stuffed everything back. The hell with refolding them neatly.

She proceeded to unzip the red suitcase and pull out its contents. Her silky undies were soon piled on top of the blue suitcase, from where they kept slipping off and falling onto the gravel road. Damn!

She was just shaking the dust off a skimpy pair of bright red panties, when a black pick up truck rumbled up the road and came to a halt beside them.

A man—actually a Greek god reincarnated—hopped down, grinning widely. "Were you trying to flag me down with those? Well, you succeeded."

Of course he'd seen the panties. Quickly she scrunched them up in her fist and slipped them into the suitcase.

"You must be Mrs. Lawrence," he said and extended his hand to help her up, but she remained crouched beside the suitcase, stuffing in the rest of her undies at lightning speed. "Hope you haven't been waiting too long."

To save the last tatters of her dignity she stood up on her own and straightened her back. With her chin rather higher than normal, she finally offered her hand. "Yes, I'm Christina Lawrence." His grip was firm and strong and she felt the calluses on his palm.

"And you, young man, are—?" The man tried to peek around her at Christopher who was crouching behind her back, clutching at her skin-tight jeans.

"This is Christopher, my son." Embarrassed, Tina tried to pull the boy out by the arm. Silly kid! Next thing he'd be putting his thumb into his mouth to really show what a baby he could be.

Which was exactly what he did. Mortified Tina yanked his hand, popping out the thumb. "Say hello to the gentleman." She spoke more severely than she'd intended, which, of course, made Christopher shirk away even more. With a shrug, Tina gave up on the tug-o-war. No doubt the man found the two of them pretty ridiculous.

"And you are—?" she asked. Maybe this wasn't the chief at all, but some lackey he'd sent to fetch them.

"I'm Hazard Abraham," he said.

"Did you say Hazard?" The question slipped out.

"That's right."

"So H. Perry Abraham stands for Hazard Perry Abraham?"

"You got that right," he told her. "My dad was big fan of the War of 1812 naval battles. Apparently I was named for a US naval captain."

"Interesting." And an extremely suitable name for such a good-looking fellow. Hazard. Though the parents wouldn't have known when he was born how handsome their son would grow up to be. With those eyes, dark as night, and the shining black hair combed back off his forehead . . . Wow! He was probably a hazard to all the women he met. And that was just his head. The rest of him, she could tell from the t-shirt and tight-fitting jeans, was just as hazardous.

Oops! Shouldn't have gone there! Quickly Tina looked down at the suitcases, to hide the heat she felt rising to her cheeks. She grabbed one of the handles and in a no-nonsense voice she said, "Well, shall we get going? Christopher is getting hungry."

"I've been hungry for hours!" the boy whined, and Tina wished he would stop sounding like such a baby. She'd always hated whiney kids and now her own son had turned into one. Whatever happened to her eager, intelligent, precocious little boy?

"I'm sure you won't starve," she said and handed him his travel bag. Inside were his books and crayons, which had kept him amused during the trip. Thank goodness he wasn't into football or some other physical activity that would have made it difficult to keep him in his seat.

"Well, to me you look like you're already starving, buddy," Hazard said and heaved the heavy red suitcase with ease up to the back of the truck.

Christopher nodded vigorously. "Yeah, I am."

Sure, make her sound like a neglectful mother.

"He had lunch in Big Thunder," she explained. "That's—" She glanced at her watch. "Good grief, that's seven hours ago!"

"See? No wonder I'm starving," Christopher whined.

Tina refrained from telling him to speak in a normal voice, not wanting to draw attention to what she hoped was a passing phase.

When the suitcases where loaded, Hazard lifted Christopher high up and deposited him to the back of the truck with the suitcases. "You'll ride up there, right?"

Panic filled Christopher's eyes. "I can't! There's no seatbelts!" he cried and then held his arms outstretched for Tina. "Mommy? Help me down."

"Don't worry," she reassured him. "Mr. Abraham was just joking." Wasn't he? "People are not allowed to ride at the back of a truck." She lifted him down, buckled him in the cab and climbed in herself.

"Yeah, just joking, buddy." Hazard switched on the ignition and they were off, bouncing among the pot holes.

This was even more uncomfortable than the bus. "It's already July," Tina remarked. "When will they get around to fixing these horrible potholes?"

"Probably never," Hazard said laconically. "Some

springs the frost heaves are pretty bad. This was one of the worst."

"But why wouldn't they fill them up? This is awful."

"Winter comes, the snow'll cover them up. And in the spring they'll be back again."

His attitude made her annoyed. "That's like saying, 'No use sweeping the floor, because it'll just get dirty again.' Or 'No use making the bed because you'll sleep in it tonight anyway.' That's a very lackadaisical attitude, in my opinion."

"That's right. It's your opinion," Hazard said evenly. He didn't sound as jovial as before. "Who are you to sprinkle your opinions around where they're not wanted?"

"Why, I just—" Tina snapped her mouth shut, totally taken aback by this rude comment. Did the man have no manners? Even if he didn't agree with her, he could have expressed himself more politely. She decided not to respond and make the situation even more acerbic. After all, they'd just met and would probably be dealing with each other quite often, especially in the beginning while she was getting settled.

Hazard steered the truck around a curve and there was the village. "Here we are," he announced.

"Where?" Christopher asked and pressed his nose against the window.

"Welcome to beautiful downtown Greenstone Number 58 Indian Reserve," Hazard swept his arm in an arc, taking in the handful of houses that were in view.

Christopher frowned. "How come you said Indian Reserve? Mommy said we aren't allowed to call you guys Indians."

"You guys aren't allowed to call us Indians," Hazard

said with a grin. "But we guys can call ourselves what-ever we wish. I call myself an Indian Chief."

"No kidding? That's cool." Eagerly Christopher turned to Tina. "Mommy, he's an Indian Chief."

"He's Mr. Abraham, dear," Tina corrected her son. She turned to Hazard, "Or maybe Chief Abraham?"

"Whatever works," was his cryptic reply. His voice still didn't have a friendly tone and Tina was sorry their meeting had started off on the wrong foot.

"Mr. Abraham," she began as they bumped and rumbled along the narrow road pocked with craters like the moon. "I am sorry if I made some unwelcome remarks earlier. It certainly was not my intention to be rude. I would appreciate it if you could chalk it up to my ignorance, and to being in a locale where the cus-toms are perhaps different from mine."

Hazard was silent for a few moments, making Tina afraid he wasn't going to take the olive branch she was extending.

Then he shrugged. "Sure," he said and turned to face her. His wide smile and crinkled eyes did some-thing surprising to her insides. "No problem."

Tina heaved a sigh of relief. At least he was amenable to accepting apologies, which was a good sign. She suspected there would be a few more times when apologies would be needed before she returned home to Toronto. Home? To the condo she'd bought just before they left, which she hadn't even furnished? Not exactly a home. Yet.

Tina put a hand on his arm. "Mr. Abraham, I won-der if you could drop Christopher and me at the hotel. I thought we'd stay there till we find a house."

"Did Steve Miller not tell you? That's all been

arranged. There's a house ready for you." Hazard steered the truck around a corner. "It was the previous teacher's, and the one before that, and the one before that. Oops, I should stop, or you'll think teachers don't stay here very long."

"I . . . I really had no idea—"

"Well, they don't. They usually leave after six months or so. Often less. But luckily Steve's managed to hang in for a couple of years."

He pulled up in front of a modest bungalow that looked somewhat more upscale than the rest of the homes Tina had seen so far in town. This one seemed to be standing on a basement, instead of on concrete pylons. In the back, close to the edge of the forest that rimmed the property on one side she could see a small aluminum shed that seemed to be in good repair.

After Hazard had parked the truck they got out and walked to the door.

"This is it," Hazard said. "I was inside earlier and cleaned it up a bit and put some food in the fridge. Maybe tomorrow you can buy some bedding at the Bay, unless you brought some with you."

"I have a trunk coming with bedding and towels," Tina told him. "But I'm sure we'll be fine for one night even without sheets and duvets." She put a hand on Christopher's shoulder and made her voice bright. "We'll have fun pretending we're camping. Right, honey?"

But this only made Christopher wrinkle his nose. "I'm hungry."

"I guess that's the only thing he has on his mind right now," Tina said with a forced laugh. "You say you left some food in the fridge? Thank you so very much.

I hope you kept the grocery bills, because I'll reimburse you."

"It's on the house," Hazard said with a wave of his hand. "I'll bring your suitcases in. The key is under the mat."

Tina smiled. "How very subtle." She felt much better now that the tension was gone. After all, who wanted to start a new relationship with a misunderstanding? Because that's all it had been. She hadn't said that the women on the reserve didn't sweep their floors or make their beds. That had just been a general analogy. And Hazard had probably misunderstood, assuming she was being critical of the women. She wasn't. But in a way it was good he was defensive about his people, because that probably made him a better chief.

The welcome aroma of fresh baking wafted into her nostrils when Tina opened the door. She drew in a deep breath.

"Lovely!" she exclaimed. "Did you do the baking, too?"

"As a matter of fact, I did," Hazard said and lowered the suitcases on the kitchen floor. "Muffins. I hope Christopher likes them."

"Where are they? Where are they?" the boy cried and followed his nose to a platter sitting on the counter, covered with a clean tea towel. He slipped his hand under the towel and pulled out a muffin, which he immediately stuffed into his mouth. "Yummy!" he said in a muffled voice.

"Christopher, you haven't washed your hands," Tina admonished him, but Hazard's laugher stopped her from saying more.

"Is it better he dies of hunger or deals with a few

germs?" he asked.

"Oh, all right. Just this once," Tina conceded, and watched with an indulgent smile as Christopher began to devour a second muffin. "I assume they're healthy. Oatmeal or something?"

"I put just about everything in them that I found in my kitchen," Hazard said.

"Yikes!" Tina giggled. "That doesn't sound very appetizing. I'm using my imagination and coming up with all sorts of things lying at the bottoms of bags and canisters."

"Well, not to worry. They were thoroughly baked at three-fifty for twenty minutes. Anything gross is dead."

Christopher's hand stopped half-way to his mouth. "What gross is dead?"

"Oh, spiders and things like that," Hazard said, his face serious. "Cockroaches. You know, things that live in kitchen cupboards."

"We don't have spiders in our kitchen cupboards. Do we Mommy?" the boy asked, panic in his eyes. He inspected the half-eaten muffin, almost pressing it against his glasses. "I don't see any spiders. Are there spiders in it?"

"No, honey, Mr. Abraham was just kidding." He better have been kidding or those muffins would find their final resting place in a compost bin. "Is there milk?" she asked, walking up to the fridge to check for herself.

"Yes. That carton should get you started."

It was whole milk. Tina didn't think Christopher would notice, but she was wrong.

He took a sip from his glass and crinkled up his nose. "Yuck. This tastes yucky."

In response to Hazard's questioning look she told him, "We drink one per cent or skim. He's not used to the taste of whole milk. Too creamy."

"You like ice cream, don't you?" Hazard asked the boy who had pushed the milk glass far from him on the counter.

Christopher nodded. "Yeah. Sure I do."

"Well, this is actually melted ice cream. Without all that sugar," he added, winking at Tina.

Tina snorted. The man had fed the child silly stories about spiders and cockroaches, and now was talking about melted ice cream. What next?

Christopher took a sip of the milk and nodded. "Yeah," he agreed. "It kinda tastes like that." He then gave Tina a sly, triumphant grin. "Look, Mommy, I'm drinking ice cream."

She pretended to be horrified. "And you haven't even had dinner, yet. What would Nana say?"

This sent Christopher into gales of laughter. "Yeah, Nana would be so-o upset, right?"

"She sure would. But just this once, you can have ice cream before dinner. We won't tell Nana and upset her."

While Christopher continued to munch on his third muffin and drink his "ice cream", Tina went to look at the rest of the house. Hazard followed her.

"I hope this is all right for you," he said. "It's just about the best house on the reserve. Yours and the doctor's. And Steve Miller's."

Tina stopped at the bedroom door and turned to him. "What do you mean?"

"Well, you come from down south and are used to good homes with well-ventilated basements and no mold-buildup in the corners. Right?"

"Of course!" Tina exclaimed. "But are you saying the people here live in moldy houses?"

Hazard shrugged. "Some do. That's the way things are around here."

Tina felt anger flare up inside her at his nonchalant acceptance of things. "You're the chief!" she cried. "Why don't you do something about that?"

"I plan to. But I just got elected this spring after I came back from Kingston. But let's look at the rest of the house, shall we?" He backed against the hall wall and let her pass by him.

Too close. She couldn't help brushing his muscular arm and chest with her shoulder, and felt a strong reaction pass through her. Okay, so he was handsome, and being near him could obviously be hazardous. Good thing she knew that now, and could keep her distance in any future dealings with him.

"So, is everything acceptable?" he asked as she peered into the tiny bathroom situated between the two bedrooms.

Was everything acceptable? Well, if she couldn't have a nice two-storey brownstone home with four bedrooms and four spacious baths, a rec room with a games area for Christopher . . . well, this would have to do.

"Sure, this'll be fine," she said brightly and hoped her voice didn't betray her. She wanted to sound enthusiastic about the house which, she now understood, was probably considered luxurious by the reserve standards. "I'm sure we'll be quite comfortable." What more could she say and not sound like a total liar.

"So, where in Toronto did you live?" Hazard asked as he followed her down the hall back to the kitchen.

Damn! He had to ask. She hoped he didn't know Toronto too intimately. "Rosedale," she told him, reluctantly naming the area where her parents had a large, luxurious house.

Hazard gave a low whistle. "Whew! I guess this is a huge leap down for you, then."

So he knew Toronto. "Well, we have a cottage on Georgian Bay and the guest house there is very much like this little—" Oh, God! Too late she realized what her words might sound like. She hoped he wouldn't notice how she was turning herself into a pretzel trying to undo her mistake. "It's not actually my cottage. It's my parents," she said, trying to pull the buns out of the fire. "It's very old. So you see, I'm—"

"A rich kid from a posh area of Toronto." The sarcasm in his voice was obvious. He made a courtly bow. "Greenstone Number 58 Indian Reserve welcomes Your Highness. Sorry we didn't lay down the red carpet but, dammit, we're all out of red carpeting. Only got some brown stuff left. It's called gravel."

"That is unnecessary and unkind," Tina said severely. Once again anger bubbled up inside her, but she suppressed it, making her disapproving words sound more like those of a teacher admonishing a student.

Hazard had the courtesy to look embarrassed. "You're right. That was totally beyond the pale. I'm sorry."

The man actually apologized. That was so unexpected from such a macho-looking male that for a moment Tina didn't know how to respond.

"Apology accepted." She tried her best to smile and held out her hand in a gesture of reconciliation.

A huge mistake. His grip sent sparks up to her shoulder and then down to where sparks had no business going. And goodness, wasn't he ever going to let her hand go? She couldn't very well pull it away, because that would have been rude. And would have made her look like a prissy.

"Mommy!" Christopher shouted from the kitchen. "Where are you?"

Hazard released her hand and Tina wasn't sure if she was relieved or disappointed.

"Right here, down the hall," she called. One couldn't very well get lost in this little house. Christopher came running up to the bathroom and squeezed in between them to see.

"Is this your bathroom, Mommy? Where's mine?" he asked.

"We're going to share this bathroom," Tina answered eagerly. "Won't that be fun?"

"How will that be fun?" Obviously the boy hadn't yet caught onto the hilarious possibilities of sharing a bathroom with his mother.

"Well, we can brush our teeth together," Tina offered, hoping he wouldn't realize that the single sink would make this difficult, if not impossible.

"But what if we both have to go pee at the same time?" Christopher wanted to know.

Tina glanced at Hazard who, by all rights, should have had the courtesy to look away and pretend he wasn't listening. But instead he looked on, waiting with obvious interest for her reply. Annoying man.

She hesitated. "Well, I mean . . . how often would

that actually happen?"

"But what if it does?" Christopher insisted.

Tina didn't know why she'd always thought his inquisitive nature was such a wonderful aspect of his personality. "We'll deal with it then," she snapped, wanting to bring this rather unsavory conversation to a quick end.

"You can always go outside and pee against a tree," Hazard helpfully suggested to Christopher.

The boy's jaw dropped in surprise. "Whaddya mean?"

Oh, God! Next thing the man would suggest that she go out and squat around the corner.

"I'll tell you someday," Hazard said.

"Well, well, won't we be cozy and comfy in our little house," Tina broke in cheerfully, afraid that Christopher's persistent curiosity would lead to a demonstration lesson.

The "cozy and comfy little house" had a centre hall design with an eat-in kitchen on one side of the hall and a living room on the other. At the end of the hall was a bathroom with two bedrooms on either side of it. From the kitchen a set of stairs led down to the basement, and a side door opened to the back yard.

"Honey, you have a chance to choose which bedroom will be yours," she said cheerfully, sending Christopher eagerly running from one bedroom to the other, while she and Hazard went back to the kitchen.

"I'd like to see the laundry facilities," she said.

"Will that be a deal-breaker?"

"Of course not. I just would like to see what they look like. I mean . . . where they are."

Hazard led the way down to the basement where

he had to walk with his six-foot-plus frame hunched over to avoid hitting his head on the floor joists above. "There's not much headroom," he acknowledged the obvious. "But the washer and dryer both work."

In the dimly lit basement, his black eyes gleamed dangerously. Which was ridiculous, because the man was just explaining the workings of the washer to her and not saying anything even remotely sexy.

So why did she feel as though she was going to be kissed? And why did she even entertain such thoughts? It was because whenever his hand came even close to hers, as he explained the dials, an electric current shot through her.

Had she simply been too long without sex, or what on earth was the matter with her?

Chapter Two

Tina woke the next morning, tired and listless. Her restless dreams had been filled with moldy corners, calloused palms, and dark eyes that gleamed dangerously in the dark. Not to mention muffins crawling with spiders. How could one man wreak such havoc throughout the whole night? Of course it wasn't Hazard's fault. It was all caused by her own over-active imagination.

So that's where Christopher got his fertile mind from. Not from his dad, whom he had never seen, and hadn't ever asked about . . . so far. (Knock, knock!) Henry and she had decided that since the pregnancy was a total surprise to both of them, despite their efforts to prevent such an accident, he wouldn't be obligated to keep in touch with the child, unless he wanted to. And he hadn't wanted to. Which, Tina had to admit, she found very hurtful. How could any man not want to be the father of a sweet boy like Christopher? But Henry was honourable and had kept up with the support payments, even after getting married and moving thousands of kilometres away, to work in a West Coast hospital.

Tina sat up and yawned, but when her toes met the cold linoleum floor she quickly pulled them back up and groped for the soft, lamb's wool slippers waiting by the bed. Who knew linoleum floors could be so chilly, even in July! Luckily she'd packed the slippers into one of the suitcases and not in the trunk, which would arrive today. She hoped.

Wrapped in her velour robe, she passed by Christopher's bedroom and peeked in. He was still sound asleep. Good! She could have a few moments of silence to gather her thoughts and prepare for the coming day that would be filled with a thousand things to do.

Tina sat down on one of the white, wooden kitchen chairs, covered with cushions that had several mallard ducks on them. Though Tina had nothing against ducks, she didn't relish the idea of sitting on them, and so the to-do list grew to a thousand and one, with new chair cushions added to it.

She plopped her forehead on the table. Whose idea was it to come here anyway? Oh yes, her own. Over her parents' objections—especially her mother's—she'd kept her head and filled in the application. Her mother had almost torn it from her hands when she was getting ready to mail it.

"You cannot take Christopher away," her mother had said sternly, hoping that would have an effect on her "willful" daughter. When the response had arrived, the poor woman had moped for days.

Honestly, one would have thought Tina was taking her son to some inaccessible far-off country, or the darkest rainforest of Amazon where her parents could never visit him. Luckily her dad was more reasonable and, though sad about Christopher leaving, had told

Tina she was doing the right thing.

"Despite your mother's reaction, you must follow your own heart," her dad had said.

Tina snorted. Yeah, she'd followed her heart, all right. All the way to Greenstone Number 58. She got up to see if she could operate the black coffee maker on the counter. It didn't look terribly complicated, with just an "On/Off" switch. Quite a far cry from her fancy, stainless steel programmable one at home. Luckily Hazard, probably anticipating her desire to get some caffeine into her in the morning, had left a bag of coffee on the counter so she didn't have to search for it in the cupboards. He'd also left a box of tea bags, in case that was her drink of preference. Very thoughtful of him.

As the coffee perked and filled the kitchen with its lovely aroma, Tina began to search through the cupboards for cereal and bowls. But when she remembered the carton of whole milk in the fridge, she decide to skip the cereal and opted for one of the muffins instead.

With a steaming mug of coffee in front of her, Tina sat at the table and bit into the muffin. She would have to ask Hazard for the recipe, because Christopher had really liked them. He had devoured three last night, which was surely a record. She'd been too tired to start cooking anything, or even try to locate the pots and pans, so she'd made peanut butter sandwiches for dinner. With a muffin for dessert. Not bad.

Christopher shuffled into the kitchen, wearing the shorts and t-shirt from yesterday. Last night Tina had been too tired to go through his suitcase and pick out a clean outfit for this morning. Without a word of greeting he plunked himself on a chair and gave a huge, tonsil-revealing yawn.

"Please, cover your mouth when you yawn," Tina reprimanded him. "I'm eating and that didn't look very appetizing."

"Okay." He scratched at the bites on his bare arms. "What's for breakfast?"

"I'll cook you some porridge. I saw a bag of oatmeal in the cupboard."

"With melted ice cream?" he asked, giving his mother a sly look from under his brows.

Tina smiled. "Naturally. I think that's how they all eat their porridge here at Greenstone."

Breakfast over, she got dressed while Christopher brushed his teeth, and they went out to look around. Their house was on the outskirts of the village, at the end of a gravel road that was, of course, full of pot holes. There were a couple of other houses not far from them, each with a variety of plastic toys and discarded or forgotten objects scattered around the yard.

Four or five barking dogs and as many children were already on the road, running and playing some rambunctious, noisy game. Christopher followed their activities for a few minutes.

He turned to Tina. "Can I have a dog?"

Good grief, where did that come from? "No, honey. We won't be here very long and we can't bring a dog home with us to Toronto."

"Why not?"

"Because when we go back, we'll move into our own condo, remember? No dogs allowed in the condo."

"Aw . . ." Christopher whined. "I don't wanna move into a condo."

"We've lived with Papa and Nana long enough. Now

that you're going to grade one you don't need a babysitter all day." Of course he knew that, but how would this reminder be received? She crossed her fingers in the pocket of her jeans.

Badly.

Tears flowed as Christopher broke down and wailed loudly, "I wanna live with Nana and Papa! I don't want to live in a condo."

The children down the road stopped their game to stare at him. Quickly Tina took him by the arm and steered him inside the house. Silly boy, raising such a ruckus.

She seated him on a kitchen chair and looked around for a tissue. Not finding one, she ripped off a sheet of paper towel from the roll hanging under the cupboard. "Wipe your eyes, Christopher," she said in her no-nonsense school teacher voice. "I can't believe a boy who's already turned six would behave like such a baby."

"I'm not a baby!" Christopher shouted furiously.

She knew he took great pride in having recently had his sixth birthday, which had been celebrated by his grandparents with way too much fanfare and fuss, in Tina's opinion. Much more than such a minor birthday deserved. But there'd been no stopping Nana from going all out.

There was a knock on the back screen door and Hazard peeked in. "Am I interrupting something?" he asked.

"Other than a total melt-down? No, not much," Tina replied. "Please come in, Mr. Abraham. Grab yourself a coffee, if you like. Go blow your nose in the bathroom, Christopher."

Hazard quickly took in the scene. "I thought maybe you'd like to visit the schoolhouse and see the town," he said, ignoring the sullen, tearful boy who slunk past him down the hall. "Unless you're not even the least bit curious. And, by the way," he added. "I'm not Mr. Abraham. I'm Hazard."

The woman looked so fresh and beautiful this morning as she stood there sipping her coffee, leaning her elbows on the counter, her cute behind sticking out slightly. Very sexy in her tight jeans and fitted red cotton blouse. In fact, she was much too sexy to be a teacher in a two-room school where some of the boys would be old enough to appreciate her looks.

Hazard certainly found it hard to take his eyes off her, as he poured himself a coffee—and in the process ended up sloshing some on the marbled green arborite counter. He pulled a paper towel from the roll and wiped off the spill.

Tina turned to face him. "Well, of course I'm curious to see the school. But are you sure you have time to chauffeur us around? I was thinking this morning that I really should buy a car."

He pulled up a chair and turned it around, sitting with his legs astride. "That probably won't be necessary, unless you want to go to Spruce Falls or somewhere for a change of scenery. Nothing on the reserve is so far that you need a car." He leaned his chin on his fists on the back of the chair.

"I was thinking of an emergency," she said. "Or in the winter when it's too cold for us to walk to school, or—"

Hazard interrupted her with a shake of his head. "I think he would be the only kid driven to school, no matter what the weather. I don't know if he wants that reputation."

"What reputation?" Christopher had blown his nose and returned to the kitchen.

"The reputation of being driven to school like a molly-coddled baby," Hazard said to the boy. "Would you like that?"

The boy stomped his foot indignantly. "No way! I'm no molly-coddled baby! I'm six years old!" He stood up to his full height and Hazard noted that he was quite tall for his age. But much too thin.

"Good. Then your mommy doesn't need a car," Hazard said and ruffled Christopher's hair.

"Oh, yes, your mommy does need a car to drive herself to school," Tina protested. "I'm not going to walk in the winter with all my books and stuff."

"Tsk, tsk. Too bad mommy is such a wimp," Hazard said to Christopher and was glad to hear her laugh in response. So she had a sense of humour. "Mommy could save her money and instead buy you a fishing rod."

Christopher stood with his elbows on the table, looking up at him. "Why do I need a fishing rod?"

Hazard pretended to cast a line. "Didn't you ever fish at that cottage on Georgian Bay?"

"My dad took him fishing once but he was so bored, he refused to go again," Tina explained. "Right, Christopher? You didn't like to fish with Papa."

"It was boring," the boy said wrinkling his nose. "I didn't like it."

"Too bad," Hazard said. It was obvious this subject had been the topic of several conversations in the family, and Christopher had given the expected response.

"I was going to ask you to come with me down to the lake. There's some whopping big fish at the mouth of the river."

Now Christopher's big blue eyes glimmered with interest behind his glasses. "Whopping big?"

"You bet," Hazard assured him. "We'll have to see about a rod for you. And maybe a tackle box. Then we can go and catch some of them whoppers."

"Yea!" Christopher shouted and ran around the kitchen.

Hazard noted the loving, indulgent smile on Tina's face as she looked at her son. The way to this mother's heart would certainly be through the boy.

Say what? With a start, he shook his head. What on earth had brought that on? He wasn't planning to go fishing for her heart. It was trout he was after.

Hazard swung his leg over the chair and went to put his coffee mug in the sink. "If you're done your breakfast, why don't we get going?"

They took off in his four-wheel truck and all the neighbouring children stopped their play to watch as they drove by, forming something resembling a path of honour. Hazard waved to them.

"Wave to the kids," he said to Christopher, who sat in the back. "They'll be your playmates while you're here." While you're here . . . Yeah, how long would that be? Maybe just a few months? Winter would scare the southerners off if nothing else would before that. Like unruly students. Or their parents. Or the mosquitoes. All teachers left sooner rather than later. The sinking feeling inside his chest surprised him.

"I don't wanna wave," Christopher said, shrinking back into his seat. "That kid has a yucky runny nose."

Right. Chogan did have a nice pair of candles under his nostrils. It was July but summer colds weren't uncommon.

"He just forgot to bring a tissue with him," Hazard said. "You sometimes have a runny nose, don't you?"

"Yes, but then I stay indoors. I don't go out to play, so other kids don't catch my cold." Christopher sounded like he was quoting someone. "That's what Nana said."

Nana? The way he pronounced the word, it sure sounded like this Nana was a huge presence in the kid's life.

"And Nana's right. You shouldn't go around infecting others with your cold." Too many kids here ran around with all kinds of infections, from impetigo to head lice. It didn't take too much imagination to know how Tina would react if such scourges should appear on her son.

They neared a collection of three sky-blue portables set up in close proximity to one another. Around the yard were a couple of basketball hoops—missing the netting, of course—a set of swings, plus a big red and yellow plastic climber with a slide—the kind one would find in most playgrounds anywhere in the country. And also something one wouldn't find in too many schoolyard in the country—outhouses.

"Your place of employment," Hazard said with a wave of his hand. "How do you like it? Pass the test?" He turned his head to look at Tina, so he could see her reaction. She didn't look stunned, which was a good sign.

"I had some idea of what the school looked like here at Greenstone," she said, unclipping her seatbelt. "I saw photos and read up on it, so I knew what to expect."

But as they walked closer to the buildings, a frown appeared on her forehead.

"Who's in charge of keeping the portables in good repair?" she asked. "The paint is chipping and the corners are broken. Kids could rip their clothing, or even their hands and heads on those projecting splinters. Why aren't they fixed?"

"Probably vandals have been hammering at the building over the summer," Hazard said."It's hard to keep up with the repairs."

"I'm sure there are men on the reserve who could do the job," Tina said and ran her fingers along the sharp protrusions on the corner of one building. "This is totally unacceptable."

"You're right. I'll get to it first thing tomorrow," Hazard said sharply. "Thank you for pointing it out to me. Anything else I can fix while I'm at it?" The woman obviously wasn't one to hold back her criticism. The roads and the portables were already in her crosshairs. What next?

Tina looked at him through narrowed eyes. "I see you are treating this lightly," she said sternly. "But I don't see it as a joke. If a child comes to me with a bleeding head wound, I won't think it's funny."

"And how many such bleeding head wounds have you treated so far at Greenstone?" Hazard couldn't keep the tightness from his voice.

"That question doesn't even make sense," Tina retorted.

Hazard winced. Things were heading in the wrong direction. He'd wanted it to be a tour of the reserve and not an argument about the portables. If she was going to be this critical about every little thing, maybe he should just cut the demonstration short and take her and her son back to the safety of their house, away from all these dangerous splinters.

Silently they walked around the buildings, and he could sense from her tightly pursed lips that Tina was trying to contain her anger. She ran a hand across one of the window panes—filthy, of course—and wiped her fingers on the back of her jeans. On her cute butt.

"Yeah," Hazard said before she could say anything. "They need a wash. Before school starts they'll be cleaned, don't worry."

"I wasn't worrying. At least I know how to squirt Windex as well as the next person. It's the carpentry repairs I'm not good at."

"Windex is expensive around here," he said, but couldn't help admiring her pluck.

"Ammonia or vinegar, then." She turned to walk toward the playground. "I hope there are no sharp edges on the equipment."

"There probably are, but we don't wrap our kids in bubble wrap. They learn to look out for dangers." Was he asking for it again? Probably.

"That so?" Silently she inspected the slide and climber. "Probably a good thing," she said quietly. "Life is full of unexpected splinters."

"That's what they said way back in the Middle Ages. Don't get pricked by the thorn hiding under a rose. Some people are like that. Thorny."

Tina cocked one eyebrow at him. "You are not, by any chance, referring to someone around here, are you?"

Hazard grinned. "Touché." Yes, she probably hid a thorn or two. But she was also very fascinating, in a challenging sort of way. He liked challenges.

Tina smiled back at him. And it was as though the sun had suddenly moved over to that side of the sky. He felt something flip inside his chest, right around the spot where he always imagined his heart was situated.

He coughed and changed the subject. "By the way, I assume you've already been in touch with the principal, Steve Miller?"

Tina shook her head. "His name was on the application form, but that's all."

"Yeah, well, he's also the junior and intermediate teacher. He's away in Big Thunder at the moment but should return soon."

"Before school starts, I hope," she joked.

Hazard didn't want to tell her that Steve Miller wasn't his most favourite person on this planet. It was strictly his own opinion and he didn't want to influence her first impressions of the man by voicing his bias.

"By the way, you asked what else you could fix," Tina said.

"Yes?"

"Those outhouses are really smelly."

Hazard raised his hands in defence and laughed. "Not my department, I'm afraid. I don't know anything about disinfecting outhouses and what's more, I don't plan to learn any time soon."

"Too bad." Tina shrugged. "They really are awful. And I don't relish the thought of having to use one."

Hazard hadn't though of that, and he didn't like the idea either. That could drive her away faster than any unruly kid. But he had no reply for her, so instead he called to Christopher who had climbed to the top of the slide, "Hey, Christopher, you want to see a wolf?"

"A wolf?" Christopher slid down and ran up to them. "Like in a zoo?" he asked eagerly.

"Actually, it's just half a wolf," Hazard said.

"Half a wolf! That's crazy. Is it dead?"

"Nope. Totally alive."

Christopher jumped up and down. "I wanna see it!" He turned to Tina. "Can we, Mommy?"

Tina raised an eyebrow and looked askance at Hazard. "You're sure this isn't going to be unpleasant? I never inspect road-kill because I have zero carrion-tolerance."

"No road-kill," he assured her. "Let's get in the truck."

Hazard drove down a couple of roads and pulled into his driveway. They got out and he led them around the corner of the house to the back yard.

"Whose yard are we entering without permission?" Tina asked, looking at the windows, as though waiting for the owner's head to appear.

"Mine," Hazard replied. "And I give us permission."

A huge cage was in a corner of the yard, close to the forest that lined the back of the lot. The animal in the cage started to howl loudly as soon as it caught sight of Hazard and its bushy tail wagged furiously.

"Howdy, buddy," Hazard called to it. "I've brought you some visitors. Behave yourself now."

Christopher dashed up to the cage. "Is it a real wolf?"

Hazard unhooked a leash that hung on a hook, opened the cage and entered. He clipped the leash onto the animal's collar and came out, leading it. "It's half a real wolf. The other half is real dog."

"Careful, Christopher!" Tina shouted in alarm as the wolf-dog began to lick Christopher's hand. "Is that dangerous?" she asked Hazard.

"It's as tame as a rabbit," he said. "Don't worry."

"Yeah, that's what they all say!" Tina retorted. "Before their rabbit takes a huge chunk out of your thigh." She pulled Christopher a safe distance away from the animal.

"It's okay, Tina. I wouldn't let anything hurt your son."

At his words Tina looked up at him with big, brown eyes that jolted his chest again, right in that same spot as before. And then she smiled, a bright smile that almost sent him down on his knees.

"What's his name?" Christopher asked, putting out his hand again for a lick.

"His name is . . . drum roll please . . . Wolf."

"Oh, how clever!" Tina cried, clapping her hands.

Hazard had to laugh. Her gentle sarcasm made him want to pick her up and swing her around. Which would have been the dumbest thing he could ever do, so instead he let Wolf lick her hand.

"Why does he lick?" Christopher put out his other hand to get more licks. He giggled. "It tickles."

"It's the wolf in him," Hazard told him. "My other dogs don't ever lick my hand."

"Wow! You have other dogs, too?" Christopher cried with obvious envy. "My Mommy won't let me have even one little puppy." He looked from under his brows at Tina, who pursed her lips at him and shook her head.

"Maybe Mommy knows how much work it is taking

care of a puppy," Hazard said. "An older dog would be much less trouble."

Christopher kicked at a stone. "She won't even let me have an old dog," he muttered.

"Honey, you know we aren't going to stay here very long and we can't bring a dog back with us." She turned to Hazard. "When we get back home we'll be moving out of my parents' house into a condo I just purchased. Dogs aren't allowed in there."

How come her words always seemed to have an uncanny way of jolting that spot in his chest?

"I told you I don't wanna live in a condo!" Christopher yelled and stomped his foot. "I want a dog!"

This subject had obviously been discussed before. Furiously.

Tina's face closed up and became the picture of embarrassed severity. "We'll talk about this at home, Christopher," she said evenly. "Mr. Hazard does not want to see or hear a tantrum in his garden."

"Actually it's Wolf who doesn't like tantrums," Hazard said. "He gets upset. See?"

The dog's tail was wagging furiously and it nuzzled and licked Christopher's hand in an effort to calm the situation.

The boy patted Wolf's head. "I'm sorry, Wolf. I didn't mean to upset you."

Hazard observed the way Christopher fondled the dog's head and scratched behind its ears. It looked like he had his heart in the right place as far as animals were concerned.

"You know what? I have an idea, if your mom approves," Hazard aimed questioning eyes at Tina.

"Can't hurt to hear it," she said. She looked pleased

with the way he'd handled her son's tantrum and it made him feel pretty satisfied with himself.

"I think Christopher's right. He should have a dog."

Tina's smile turned into a frown. "Wait a minute! Didn't you hear me say that—"

Hazard put up a defensive hand. "Yes, I heard you, but now please hear me out. Okay?"

With a grimace she nodded reluctantly. So she wasn't a totally unreasonable woman.

"Christopher, what if I let you borrow a dog until you leave?" Until you leave . . . These southerners, they only stayed so long. Nothing new there. So why did this thought now cause his stomach to sink?

"Whaddya mean?" Christopher asked.

Yes, what exactly do you mean by that? Tina's one raised eyebrow and firmly crossed arms also asked him.

"Well, you can choose a dog from the ones I have. You keep it at your house, and you take care of it. It's your dog until you leave. Then it comes back to me."

Christopher's eyes shone. He grabbed a hold of Tina's hand and squeezed it. "Mommy, can I? Can I, please?"

"Well, let's see the dogs first. Then—"

"Where are they?" Christopher jumped around. "Can I see them? Oh boy, oh, boy, oh boy!"

Hazard let them into his house, trying to remember if he'd left the breakfast dishes in the sink, or scattered around on the table and the counter. He definitely knew hadn't washed them. Damn.

As soon as they entered, two dogs eagerly ran forward to greet him. One of them came up to Christopher, wagging its tail, and poked him on the arm.

"He's asking you to play," Hazard said.

Grinning broadly, the boy rubbed and scratched its pointy ears. The smaller dog politely sniffed the guests and then lay down to continue its nap.

"I like this dog," Christopher enthused. "What's his name?"

"Mutt. And I see he likes you, too." His eyes met Tina's over the boy's head. Would she agree?

"What kind of a dog is it?" she wanted to know. "It looks like a husky, but—"

"It's a Heinz 57. So is Jeff, here, who kind of looks like a—"

"A Cocker Spaniel," Christopher broke in. "I've got lots of books about dogs. I know what Heinz 57 is, too. It's like lots of dogs mixed up together into one dog."

Hazard had to smile at this eagerness. "That right. And I guess you know a lot about caring for dogs, too?"

"Yup! I know everything," Christopher announced grandly. He looked up at his mother. "Please may I borrow him, Mommy?" he asked sweetly.

Hazard didn't know how anyone could refuse anything those big, blue eyes asked for. And obviously Tina couldn't, either.

"All right," she finally said. "I'll probably rue the day I agreed to this, but yes, you may borrow Mutt."

Christopher started to run around the house, whooping and hollering, with Mutt following close behind. Hazard saw Tina's mouth open to stop this jubilation, but with a slight shake of his head he signaled her to just let the boy rejoice.

After wearing off some of his excitement, Christopher sat on a rug on the living room floor and Mutt placed its head on his lap.

"Mommy, can Mutt sleep in my bed?" he asked.

"Absolutely not!" Tina cried. "No dogs on beds."

Looked like another confrontation was brewing between the mother and son. Hazard placed a hand on Christopher's head. "I have an idea," he proposed. "How about you and I build Mutt a dog house? Then he can sleep outside which is where he really likes to sleep, anyway. I left him inside today only because there were rumours of a black bear roaming around the garbage dump." This last part he addressed to Tina.

"Yes! Let's build it right now!" Christopher yelled, totally ignoring what Hazard had said about the bear.

But obviously Tina hadn't. She looked at him in alarm. "A bear? Around here?"

"They come sometimes. No one's ever been hurt," Hazard hurried to reassure her. "No need to worry." He didn't want her to overreact and curtail her son's movements, because the kid seemed to be in need of a bit of independence. "We'll build it soon," he said to Christopher. "But today I wanted to take you and your mom around the town."

Chapter Three

Over Christopher's objections they left Mutt in the house, and continued the tour. Tina looked eagerly at all the children she saw. In September she'd be welcoming them into her classroom. She was also keen to see their homes and looked with interest at the houses they passed.

Hazard pointed out a rather opulent house surrounded by a black wrought iron fence.

"Now, that's different!" Tina exclaimed.

"Yes, that's the home of the previous chief," Hazard said. "It's pretty classy, by village standards."

"How come?"

"I guess he used the funds . . . " Hazard seemed to be choosing his words carefully. "He made sure he had the means to live in style."

"What funds?" Tina stared at the long RV parked on the front lawn.

"Every reserve gets funds from the Federal Government, and—"

"Yes, I realize that," Tina broke in. "So are you saying he lined his pockets with—?"

Hazard frowned. "I'm not saying anything. Nothing's

been proven and it's just being investigated."

"But that's horrible!" Tina burst out. It sounded like the chief had purloined the government money meant for his people and left them to live in what looked to her almost like shacks. "Is that why they chose you for their new chief?"

"I think they chose me because I just graduated with a business degree from the university." He glanced at the back seat where Christopher was soaking in every word, and lowered his voice. "I didn't continue my education right after high school. I just hung around for a good decade or more, like most of my friends, till my parents told me to smarten up. So I applied to the university in Kingston as a mature student. I got in, graduated, and here I am. The new chief."

"And you'll do better, won't you?" Christopher put in.

Tina smiled and shook her head. Obviously, despite Hazard's lowered voice, her son had heard and, what's more, had understood every word.

"You'll fix up the school, right?" Christopher asked.

Hazard winked at him over his shoulder. "Of course I will."

They continued to drive around the reserve and Hazard pointed out the building where the band council met, which also housed his office. He drove past the Hudson's Bay store as well as the town's recreation centre.

"We show movies there every Saturday. And we flood the rink in the winter." Hazard looked back at Christopher. "I guess you can skate, eh?"

"I sure can!"

"And play hockey?"

"No," the boy replied sullenly. "Mommy won't let me. She says I'll get hurt."

Tina grimaced. Sure, make her sound like an over-protective parent. Which she probably was. Kind of. "There's so much violence in hockey," she hastened to explain. "Concussions and broken bones and smashed-in teeth. I just don't see how that can be considered a healthy activity for children. Surely a child can skate without playing hockey."

To her relief, Hazard nodded. "Can't argue with that."

Tina could have kissed him, while Christopher fell back in his seat, stymied, his head sunk between his shoulders.

True to his word, Hazard came to the house the next day with Mutt, and brought with him all the materials for building the doghouse. Before Christopher went out, Tina thoroughly sprayed him with insect repellent.

"Hazard doesn't use insect repellent!" he grumbled.

"Christopher does," Tina stated firmly. "I don't want to hear you whining about itchy arms tonight."

"I don't whine," he whined.

"You just did, buckaroo."

Christopher grabbed his drawing pad, on which he had carefully designed plans for a doghouse, and ran out to show Hazard. Soon Tina heard sawing in the backyard through the screened-in open kitchen window, followed by loud hammering. Obviously Christopher was at work because most of the blows sounded like they connected with wood, with very few clinks that signified a hit on a nail. But that didn't seem to daunt him, and each time the metal-to-metal sound rang out, she could hear his satisfied, "Yeah."

By lunch time the house was beginning to take shape and only wanted a roof. Tina was glad Hazard was taking his time and letting Christopher do all the measuring, most of the hammering and even some of the sawing, using an old-fashioned hand saw.

"Come in, Master Carpenters, and have a sandwich," Tina called out to them through the back screen door. She wasn't keen to go out among the mosquitoes and flies.

The sandwiches disappeared quickly, and afterwards, while Christopher played outside with Mutt, Tina and Hazard sat at the kitchen table finishing their coffee.

"You don't know how grateful I am to you for all you're doing with Christopher," she began. "I don't remember when he was this excited about a project."

"How come? Didn't his father do stuff with him?"

She realized Hazard wasn't familiar with Christopher's history and for a while she debated whether to tell him. He knew Tina had come here alone, but that was as far as his knowledge of her went. Nothing in her files indicated whether she was widowed or divorced. Or a single mother, for that matter. After all, was it anyone's business? But she wanted Hazard to know, because somehow she knew he wouldn't broadcast it as gossip around the reserve.

"Christopher never knew his father," Tina said. Should she elaborate? She decided not. "We've been living with my parents since he was born and my father isn't exactly a jack-of-all-trades. When anything needs doing, he calls a tradesman."

"That's too bad."

What, exactly did that statement mean? Too bad about Christopher not knowing his father, or too bad her father wasn't a jack-of-all-trades. She decided it meant the latter and went on. "That's why Christopher can't hit a nail on the head." She laughed. "Except once in a while by mistake."

Hazard smiled. "Can you?"

"Nope. I freely admit it, so you don't have to put me to a test."

She liked the way his eyes crinkled when he smiled. But she also liked to see those black eyes looking at her in a way that told her he thought she was attractive. And she wondered if he saw the same admiration in her eyes, because she couldn't deny he was hazardously handsome.

But was he married? He had a nice house, but nothing had been said about there being a woman in it. She assumed there wasn't, but it wouldn't hurt to make sure.

"You're so good with children, I'm wondering if you have any of your own?"

Hazard's booming laughter rang out. "Now, if that isn't a leading question—"

"Your question was just as leading, Mr. Abraham," Tina riposted, trying to sound indignant, but had to laugh instead. "Okay, I guess we should come clean about ourselves so we don't have to do any more fishing."

"I'll start. I'm not married. Not divorced, either. And since I just got back this spring from Kingston where I was for five years, I haven't even had time to find a girlfriend."

"So, are you looking?" If she were staying she wouldn't have minded filling that role.

"I guess a guy's always looking. Nobody wants to be alone every night."

Tina blushed. This was straying into much too intimate territory, but it was her own fault for asking. She lowering her gaze. "I'm sorry. I didn't mean to—"

"But what could be more important?" he said, his voice a low rumble. "That's what life's all about."

Tina felt a thrill spike up her spine. He lived up to his name. He was hazardous. But when he reached across the table and took her hand in his, she froze. Just because she'd told him about Christopher's father, was he thinking she was free game?

"Please don't touch me," she snapped and yanked her hand away, hiding it on her lap.

Hazard's eyebrows shot up in surprise. He pulled his arm back, picked up his coffee cup and took a gulp.

How stupid of her to attack him, especially since she'd brought up the subject herself. Embarrassed and angry at her own behavior, she stared at the table. "Just because I told you I had Christopher out of wedlock, please do not ever imagine that I am ready to jump into bed with just anyone," she muttered defensively.

"I never thought that," Hazard said. His voice was not defensive, nor betraying any anger he may have felt at her words. "I'm sorry if you mistook my gesture. And I certainly didn't mean to make you angry."

Tina brushed a strand of hair off her face and sighed. "You didn't." She shook her head and then looked up into his eyes. "I'm angry at myself. I don't usually talk about my past. Nor do I ask personal questions. And I also don't normally fly off the handle like that. I'm so very sorry." She put out her hand. "I should be thanking you for being so kind to Christopher instead of lambasting you."

He grasped her hand. "It's all good," he said and his eyes crinkled in that hazardous way he had.

For a few moments, she let her hand remain in his. It felt good to have it enclosed like that in his.

"Thank you," she then said and got up to stand at the counter. She looked out the window above the sink at Christopher who was playing in the backyard with Mutt.

Hazard joined her. "He needs some playmates. And you need some friends, too. Women friends," he added with a meaningful, sly grin.

The significance of his words made an easy laugh bubble out of her. This didn't feel at all like he was getting too close or personal. Instead it felt nice to think he was being slightly—although humorously—protective of her. And protection was something she probably would need while getting used to this new, strange environment.

Protection. Which made her remember what he'd said yesterday about the bear that was prowling in the vicinity. She now turned to him with a concerned frown.

"Is Christopher safe out there by himself? I mean, with the bear and all?"

"Mutt will signal if a bear or anything else approaches. I'll go over some safety routines with him concerning wild animals. He'll be okay."

But she was definitely not okay. "Bears or . . .?" she asked suspiciously. "What else can come out of the woods?"

"I was thinking maybe a coyote."

Tina grasped the edge of the counter and her eyes scanned the forest that started right at the edge of the backyard. "Of course you would have them here. There are some even in Toronto, with a population in the millions."

"Good, then he's used to coyotes."

"No!" she cried. "Of course he's not used to coyotes. He's never seen one."

"That's okay. Please don't get upset. He's always going to have Mutt with him. And as long as he never goes deep into the bush by himself, he'll be okay. Wild animals don't often wander right into town."

"Often?"

"Well, you just said yourself there are coyotes even in Toronto with a population of millions. We have exactly four hundred and fifty-three people on the reserve." He held up two fingers. "Four hundred and fifty-five now, with you and Christopher."

Two of the children from up the road had wandered into the backyard. They were patting Mutt and Tina saw their unkempt hair was stringy and dull, indicating it hadn't been washed recently. Or maybe not with a very good shampoo. Christopher moved slightly aside to give them room beside Mutt.

"Hazard," Tina began cautiously, not wanting to spoil the easy friendship they had just established after her outburst. "Those children . . ."

"Yes. James and Chogan. Nice kids."

"But do they have—um—pediculosis?"

"I don't think so. They've been vaccinated," Hazard replied with a straight face.

Tina gave his arm a reprimanding slap. "Cut that out! You know I mean head lice."

"I know. Some of them might, of course. Just like, I might add, kids in Toronto, your city of millions. I don't know about your posh part of town but—" His voice had again taken on a defensive edge.

"Forget my posh part of town," Tina interrupted. "I'm only trying to understand what the health issues are around here."

At that Hazard relaxed visibly, and Tina breathed a sigh of relief. Another confrontation avoided.

"You're right. Now that they're not in school, the lice don't get around that easily," he said. "So I think you can relax about that lousy issue. But it's probably prudent to check his hair if he starts to scratch, just like in—"

"Toronto," she finished off for him. "I know."

Christopher ran in, followed by two boys who came to a sharp stop at the door and stood, shyly leaning against the doorframe.

"These kids came to say hello to Mutt. They're James and Chogan. And Mutt already knows them," Christopher announced.

Tina went over and smiled at the boys. "Hello, James and . . . Chogan? Is that right?"

One of the children nodded but neither one smiled back.

"Chogan is an Algonquin name," Hazard explained. He turned to the boys. "So how are you guys? Enjoying the summer?"

Both kids now smiled broadly. "Yeah," the one

called Chogan said in a deep voice that sounded grown-up compared to Christopher's chirping. The other boy simply nodded.

"We're gonna build a house and live in it!" Christopher enthused. "We're gonna cook food and everything!"

"Those are pretty big plans," Tina marveled. "And where is this house going to be built?" She was delighted to see Christopher so enthusiastic. It had brought roses onto his pale cheeks and made his big blue eyes sparkle behind his glasses.

"In the forest! We're gonna use branches."

"Oh no!" Tina couldn't help the cry from escaping and immediately felt bad for the three children who looked at her in bewilderment. "I don't want you to go into the forest," she explained. Talk about sounding lame.

Christopher puckered his brow. "Why not?" He then turned to Hazard. "We can go into the forest, can't we, Hazard?"

Tina felt a jolt of anger inside her. Her son was stepping over her and looking to Hazard as a higher authority.

"Well, you all know that bear's been prowling around the garbage dump," Hazard began. "So it's probably better if you guys stay on the edge of the bush and don't go too far in."

Tina felt her cheeks heat up. She had been intending to tell them that very same thing, if he hadn't opened his mouth first and made himself look like Big Chief Know-it-all!

With nods of assent the boys turned to go and soon were breaking off the lowest, spindly branches of some of the trees.

"You know the expression, 'Give and inch and they'll take a foot'," Tina said and couldn't keep the stern edge off her voice.

"Meaning . . .?"

"Let them go to the edge of the forest and next thing they'll be right inside it."

"We call it the bush around here," Hazard said. "It doesn't really deserve to be called a forest. As you can see, it's kind of spindly. Not exactly a robust forest."

"That is not my point!" Tina cried in exasperation. How infuriating could the man be!

"I got your point. I just pointed out something else." Hazard spoke calmly and soothingly. It was obvious he wanted to avoid a confrontation over this matter.

But she wasn't above starting an argument to make her case, not when it concerned Christopher's safety. "What if they go into the forest and get attacked by a coyote? Or a bear? Then what?"

"The boys know what to do."

"But Christopher doesn't!" she almost yelped.

"Tina, calm down. One—they are in the yard and haven't gone into the bush. And two—if they do, all the kids on the reserve have been taught what to do, and what not to do, if they meet a wild animal."

Tina snorted. "How comforting." She turned away from the window to face Hazard defiantly, arms akimbo.

"I don't want you to worry," he said quietly.

But that failed to make her feel comforted.

Hazard wanted to take her in his arms and kiss away the frown that marred her beautiful face. But of course that would have been the last thing he would ever get to do with her, because she would drum him out of her life so fast he wouldn't see what hit him.

And of course he wasn't seriously thinking of kissing her. He was simply dreaming of it. Dreaming about it a lot these last couple of days, it seemed. Chief Crazy Fool.

Christopher dashed into the kitchen again, followed by Mutt. "We need a saw!" he yelled, out of breath with the importance of his mission. "We have to cut some of them branches shorter."

"Well, you know we left the saw in the shed," Hazard said. "Go get it."

Horror was reflected on Tina's face as she listened. She raised a hand to stop her son, but he was already out the door and the arm fell listlessly to her side.

"What are you doing?" she whispered. "You're saying it's okay for him, at the age of six, to use dangerous tools?"

How could he stop her from having all these unnecessary fears? "I showed him how to handle the saw this morning. He's okay with it. I promise."

And right on cue, as a consequence of his prophetic words, a shrill scream came from the yard. It was immediately followed by the loud thumping of three pairs of feet stomping up the back stairs.

Damn. Of course it had to happen. Hazard groaned inwardly, as the boys burst into the kitchen, led by Christopher who was wailing and grasping his left hand, blood oozing through his fingers.

Tina grabbed a terry towel from the cabinet door and fell on her knees in front of her son. She wrapped it around his hand to stanch the bleeding.

Over Tina's shoulder Hazard saw the jagged wound slashed across Christopher's palm, as she opened up the towel to get a closer look at the cut. She rewrapped the blood-soaked towel around it and looked up at him. "We have to get him to the clinic. He needs stitches."

"You're right. We have to get that stitched up," he said, playing for time while he tried to think of a plan. "It could get infected now that it's summer. Besides, it's difficult to keep a cut on the palm closed up with just a bandage."

"Thank you for your diagnosis, Doctor Abraham," Tina snapped. "Now could you very quickly drive us to the clinic, please?"

He knew it was worry that made her speak so curtly, plus the fact that Christopher hadn't stopped screaming.

"I'll call Dr. Matthews and tell him we're on our way. Unfortunately he's at Red Lake today." He waited for the explosion and, sure enough, it came.

"You mean to tell me he's not at the clinic?" Tina cried. "How far away is this Red Lake?"

"Seventy-five kilometres," Hazard told her. "So we should get going. But before that, you better pour some hydrogen peroxide on the cut. The saw blade was dirty."

"I don't have any damned hydrogen peroxide," Tina stated, her voice dangerously low. "And what's more, I don't have a damned car."

"I have both. We'll pick some up at my place on the way. Let's go."

Outside Hazard asked James and Chogan to take care of Mutt. He then picked Christopher, who hadn't stopped crying, up in his arms and deposited him in the back seat of his truck with his mother.

It would be a long, noisy drive.

On the way back home luckily Christopher fell asleep in the back seat, which was a relief, after the wailing and whimpering they'd had to suffer through the entire seventy-five kilometres to Red Lake. His little palm had a dozen stitches and was neatly bandaged.

Something was brewing with Tina, who sat beside Hazard, silent as a sphinx. She looked out the window at the passing scenery, which wasn't much to look at, with her hands clutched tightly on her lap.

After a few kilometres she finally opened up. "Now, what did you say about me not needing a car? Something about everything being close enough to walk? Isn't that what you said?" Her voice was dripping with sarcasm.

"I was there to help, wasn't I?"

"And you'll always be right there, whenever I need you?"

Although this was also said in the same aggressive tone, Hazard wanted to tell her that yes, he wanted to always be there for her. Instead he said, "Someone will always be able to take you wherever you wish. If not me, then someone else with a vehicle."

"So what's wrong with me having my own vehicle? I'm used to being able to get in a car and drive wherever I wish. A car is . . . it's independence. I can't be without a car."

Hazard understood. After what she'd told him about moving away from her parents' home into a place of her own, he guessed she was trying to show herself and her parents that she could manage on her own. Probably this job was a part of that plan.

And he could only admire her for that. "So we'll get you a car, then."

"I can get my own car. Where do they sell cars around here?"

"In Big Thunder."

"Which is four hundred kilometres away!"

"Yes." He grinned. "You and Christopher can always hitchhike there and drive back."

But Tina didn't even crack a smile at his feeble attempt at humour. She was probably too proud to ask him to drive her, so Hazard knew he would have to do the offering.

"I can drive you there on Saturday when I'm not working. Or if you can't wait, I can ask someone else—"

"I can wait," she said shortly. And then, almost as an after-thought, she snapped, "Thank you."

But she continued to sit mutely, a sure sign that she wasn't through. After a few more kilometres admiring the scruffy spruce, she turned to him.

"I have been waiting for you to say something," she began stiffly.

"Like . . .?"

"Like you're sorry you gave the saw to a little child."

Hazard knew he would have to choose his words carefully, but he didn't want to give her the wrong impression, either. He had no problem with kids using sharp tools, as long as they'd been shown how to do it correctly. "I am sorry, but I'm not sorry about that," he said. "I'm sorry he got hurt."

Her incredulous eyes threw daggers at him. "You mean you would do it again?"

"Of course. The sooner the better. It's like falling off a horse. You have to get back on as quickly as possible."

"So he can slice himself again? I can't believe I'm hearing this."

"He won't slice himself again. He knows better now."

"You think so, do you?" She snorted. "So what weapon do you have in mind to give him next?"

"A knife. I was thinking of showing him how to use a knife, if he doesn't know already." This conversation was not going well. He wanted so much to get along with this woman, but whenever they talked, it seemed things always got acerbic.

Tina's sarcastic laughter filled the car. "Sure, he knows how to use a knife. And he's really great with handguns, too. You know these Toronto kids." She slapped her forehead. "Oh, my Lord! You are unreal."

"The kids on the rez are pretty handy with all kids of tools. Christopher will want to learn, too." Hazard expected this statement to get a negative reaction. It did.

"Well, I do not want him to be like the other kids on the rez—as you call it. I do not want him running around with unwashed hair, probably full of lice, with his nose running, and dirt under his fingernails. Not my son!"

"That's too bad."

Chapter Four

Tina knew she'd gone too far. Hazard's jaw was set and his mouth was drawn into a tight line. He always became defensive whenever she said anything negative about how things were on his reserve. Like when she made those comments about the school, or about pediculosis. And now she'd totally maligned the children of the village, placing her son above them.

Not very nice of her.

She sat for a few minutes, gathering her courage. Then she coughed and took a deep breath.

"Hazard, I'm sorry," she began, keeping her tone as contrite as possible. "What I just said was very unkind. It's not how a teacher should think about her students. You must consider me totally unsuitable to teach the children of the reserve. I know I sounded like a . . . like a—"

"Prejudiced snob."

Tina almost hit the roof. "I am not a snob!" she cried. "And I am not prejudiced! I value all people. To me it makes no difference what colour they are, or what their sexual preference is. And I don't just tolerate different races and nationalities, I accept them. As people. As human beings."

But she definitely had her limits in matters of personal hygiene where—she had to admit—she was quite
particular. Okay, priggish even.

Her words failed to impress Hazard, who sat stonily
beside her. In profile he looked very much the stereotypical Indian. A handsome Indian. A sexy-as-hell Indian.

"It's just that you must admit those two boys do
look somewhat scruffy, if you know what I mean." Did
she sound like a prig?

Obviously she did.

"One person's scruffy can be another person's idea
of neatness," he said evenly.

"Oh, really!" Tina exclaimed and then turned down
her volume when Christopher stirred in the back seat.
"You can't tell me they were in their Sunday best this
morning."

"It's not Sunday, is it?"

This was going so badly Tina almost cried. Why
didn't he try to be reasonable? Those boys were dirty
and unkempt and there was no way anyone could say
they weren't. It was a fact, as plain as the candles
under Chogan's nose. But she knew she would never
get Hazard to agree, because he was obviously in his
Big-Chief-Defending-His-People mode. She huffed and
shrank down, head between her shoulders.

There was silence in the car for several kilometres
while Tina chewed a fingernail down to nothing and
tried to think what she could say that he wouldn't take
the wrong way.

"So will you really come with me to find a car this
Saturday?" she at last asked, turning in her seat toward him

so he could see that her face was friendly.

"Of course. But you can do some legwork before we go and Google some used car dealers in Big Thunder to see what's available, and—"

"Oh, I don't trust used cars. I was thinking of a Lincoln sedan," Tina broke in. "That's what my dad always drives and he swears by them."

Hazard whistled. "Yes, that's a nice car all right," he said. "But I think on these rutted roads it may be better to buy a more sturdy four-wheel. And since money doesn't seem to be an object, I would recommend an SUV."

"Sure," Tina agreed. "If you think that would be better."

No wonder Christopher looked up to Hazard for opinions. He sounded so knowledgeable that she found herself doing the same. But did she really have a choice? Cars weren't exactly her thing and she'd always followed her father's advise.

"Okay, we'll go in a couple of weeks, if you can hold out that long. I'm going fishing next weekend," Hazard said. "But just be ready to stay the whole day, since the drive itself will take at least four hours."

Tina pursed her lips. So his fishing was more important than her car? "Well, I can only hope I won't have another emergency in that time."

"Not likely," Hazard reassured her. "And besides, I'm always here for you."

Right. They were such nice, comforting words. Coming from such a strong, comforting man. But she wasn't here to start leaning on anyone. Not even on such nice, broad shoulders like his.

"And you're okay driving home by yourself in your

new vehicle?" Hazard asked. His words sounded con-
descending and further upped her resolution to not
depend on him any more than absolutely necessary.

"Of course." She tried not to sound too haughty.
"I'm used to driving long distances by myself."

"Are we getting a new vehicle, Mommy?" Christopher had awakened and got right into the conversation. "When?"

"Not for a while," Tina replied. Drats! Too bad he'd
heard them. She really didn't want to hear him chatter
about the new car for the next two weeks. "Mr. Abraham thinks we should get an SUV."

"Yea!" Christopher was about to clap his hands but
the bandages reminded him of his wound. "This doesn't
even hurt now, Mommy," he said. "Hazard, how come
this doesn't hurt?"

"The doctor froze your hand," Hazard said. "But I
don't think it's going to hurt much even after the freezing's gone. The wound is nicely cleaned and stitched
up and will heal really well. No prob."

"Good," Christopher said and sniffed his bandages.
"It smells funny."

"It's the antiseptic," Hazard told him.

And again Tina was cognizant of how much weight
Hazard's words carried. If he'd said the hand will
never, ever hurt again, Christopher would have believe
him. Which wouldn't have been such a bad thing,
would it? Hmmm . . . Could Hazard also do something
about the boy's whining . . .?

Tina had spent a couple of evenings planning how
to arrange her primary classroom, and had sketched
several designs of where her own desk would be and

how she would arrange the different grade levels. She would have liked to go and see the interior of her portable, but the keys were with a school board member who happened to be away on a week's fishing trip to a northern lake. He had pocketed them along with the rest of his keys, not thinking the new teacher just might like to take a look at her classroom.

The only buildings open to her were the outhouses, but she decided not to go near them until she had to. The smell from them had almost overpowered her when she had approached them earlier.

When the keys at last were in her hand, Tina unlocked the sky-blue portable and carefully pulled open the door. A whiff of stale, musty air quickly sent her back onto the steps, right on Christopher's toes.

"Ow!" he yelled. He was holding Mutt on a leash with his good hand, but the dog was trying to push his way into the room between Tina's legs.

"Out!" Tina cried. "Stay out, both of you, till I open some windows." She peeked cautiously into the room and saw a quick movement in a corner—the tail end of a mouse skittering under some boxes in the cloakroom area. She was sure it wasn't big enough to be a rat, although never having seen a live rat, how could she know for sure?

Tina bit her lip and promised herself she would not scream. A woman who screamed at the sight of a mouse was especially high on her list of people she never wanted to emulate. At least not in front of her son. She'd been told a dog or coyote could smell fear, but luckily a child couldn't. So although at this moment she was close to a meltdown, she did a credible job of pretending she wasn't.

Shuddering she walked gingerly across the room over to the windows, scanning the floor the whole time. The room was an unholy mess. The previous teacher had obviously left in a hurry at the end of June without bothering to tidy up, and the janitorial services at the school didn't seem to operate during the summer. So, if she wanted a clean classroom, it looked like she would have to do it herself, like some lady teacher two hundred years ago.

For a second Tina thought about asking Hazard if there was someone in charge of cleaning the portables, but he would probably take that as a criticism of that person who obviously hadn't done his or her job. She didn't want to give Hazard any opportunity to insinuate she was a spoiled city teacher who couldn't do anything for herself.

Holding her nose Tina tiptoed through the papers, books and shoes scattered on the floor, not to mention the hoodies and various pieces of dirty clothing. She tried to pull up one of the three windows that were along one wall but it didn't budge. She whacked at the frame with her palm and only managed to get a sore hand. Picking up a random running shoe from the floor, she gave the frame a few sharp knocks with the rubber heel. No luck.

After trying in vain to open the other two windows, she jammed the door open as wide at it would go, using one of the little chairs, and sat down on it to survey the scene. So much for setting up her classroom. What she needed to do first was clear the room by taking all the desks and chairs outside. Then she had to bring a broom and a dust pan, a vacuum cleaner, a huge garbage bag, and a big box for the lost and found items. What else? A bucket and a mop to scrub the floor, and a squeegee and vinegar for the windows. Plus spray disinfectant, a pair of rubber gloves, and a whole bunch of rags to wash the bookshelves, the desks and chairs, and even the closet.

Good Lord! Tina slapped her forehead. Without a car she would have to cart all the cleaning stuff from her house to the school on foot. Wasn't it lucky that everything in town was within walking distance? Too bad she didn't have a wheelbarrow.

"Let's go," she said briskly to Christopher. She left the door open and took off down the road, marching at such a quick pace that Christopher had to jog to keep up with her. Mutt, on the other hand, seemed to enjoy the romp.

"Why are we going back?" the boy whined. "I thought we're going to set up the classroom?"

"We have to clean it first," Tina replied shortly. She was furious at this turn of events, and his whining didn't help. If he would only go back to speaking in a normal voice, that would do much to raise her spirits.

It took two trips, with Christopher's reluctant one-handed help, to carry everything she needed to the school. Of course she could have asked James and Chogan, who were out on the road looking on without a word as usual, while she marched past with her vacuum cleaner, bucket and mop.

And it also might have helped if she'd been familiar with some of the people around the reserve, so she could have asked them to help. But she hadn't had time to meet anyone except Hazard and the two boys. Her nearest neighbour hadn't come to meet and greet her with a steaming casserole or a batch of cookies, and Tina hadn't felt it was up to her to make the first move. Although, who knew what the protocol was around here.

She heaved the two plastic bags, loaded with cleaning stuff, up against her chest to take the load off her arms for a bit, and stubbornly raised her chin up a few inches. She was young and strong and could manage very well on her own.

As she passed the town council offices, she heard a familiar voice calling from the doorway.

"Hey, Tina!" It was Hazard. "What are you up to? I saw you motor by earlier and here you go again."

She stopped and put the bags down. Christopher also laid his plastic bag, full of rags and a bottle of vinegar, on the road.

"We're cleaning the school!" he called out. "It's a mess! Mommy even saw a mouse. She thinks there may be a mouse nest in the closet."

"Hush, don't yell, Christopher," Tina reprimanded him in a whisper. Then she looked at Hazard. "My plan was to start setting up the room, but it needs to be cleaned first. We're just bringing all the cleaning stuff over."

Yes, Chief Abraham. Leisurely walking around town was a bit different from lugging a vacuum cleaner. However, she kept her mouth clamped shut and simply waved her hand before picking up the bags and continuing on her way.

"I wish I could come and help," Hazard called after her. "But we're in the middle of a council meeting."

"Hey, no prob!" Tina called back. "We're managing just fine."

At the portable she slipped a big rubber glove on

Christopher's bandaged hand and secured it around his wrist with some string.

"Your first job is to pick up all the clothing from the floor and hang them on the coat hooks. The shoes you can put into this big box. Then pick up all the books off the floor and pile them on the teacher's desk. I'll wash the shelves later, but first we have to clear the floor. Three jobs. You got that?"

She carried out the furniture, piling up the chairs and tables willy-nilly in the yard. When the room was empty of furniture, she grabbed the broom and began to sweep the floor. This raised such a cloud of dust that she was about to send Christopher to play outside. But instead she took one of the clean rags from the bag and approached him.

"Here. I'll tie this around your mouth and nose so you won't breathe in all this dust," she said.

Christopher backed off, like she knew he would. "No! I don't want a rag on my face!"

"It's a perfectly clean rag."

"But it's still a rag. Yuck!"

"You'd rather breathe in this dust with mouse poop in it?"

"No."

"So don't argue." And with that she quickly tied the rag to cover his mouth and nose. She knew she'd have to listen to him complain, but that was preferable to hearing him cough tonight.

After she'd swept everything into a pile, Tina picked the crayons, pencils and erasers out of the dirt pile and deposited them in a small box on the teacher's desk. She took pride in being a teacher who never threw away perfectly useable supplies.

When the floor was clear of clutter, she vacuumed it. She then looked around for water. There was no sink in the portable, but in the yard she'd seen a tap at the end of a long metal pipe sticking out of the ground. Maybe it was a drinking fountain?

She was happy to discover it actually worked, and the water looked clear enough for washing a floor. She filled a bucket, squirted in some disinfectant, and proceeded to mop the floor.

Christopher had finished his jobs and was at the playground with Mutt, sliding and climbing single-handedly.

With plenty of vinegar and elbow grease, Tina scrubbed the window panes on the outside and then repeated the process inside. Maybe the windows didn't open, but at least now she could see out.

"I think that's all we'll do today," she called out to Christopher. "We'll put the desks and chairs back in and wash them tomorrow."

Just then Hazard conveniently drove into the schoolyard in his truck. "Would you like a drive home?" he asked.

"We certainly would. Right after you help me put the desks and chairs inside." Tina swept a strand of stray hair off her forehead. She probably looked a mess, but what the heck, she'd been cleaning all day.

With Hazard's help the job was quickly done. They climbed into his truck and took off.

"Oh, there's something I need help with," Tina remembered. "The windows of the portable need to be pried open. The room needs airing, badly."

"I'll see to it on my lunch hour tomorrow," Hazard said. "But I was wondering if I could treat you to dinner tonight? You've been working hard today and probably don't feel much like cooking."

"Yea! Can we go to McDonalds?" Christopher shouted.

"Sorry, no McDonalds here," Hazard told him. "But we do have Harold's Diner. Food's really good. It's cooked by Harold's wife, Anna. She goes into the bush and picks a lot of the ingredients herself, like mushrooms and berries in the fall and fiddleheads in the spring. She also bakes bannock," he finished with a touch of pride in his voice.

Tina was determined this dinner would not turn into a confrontation. "Sounds fantastic. Maybe you could pick us up at the house in a couple of hours?"

She still found it difficult to say "home". Maybe once she changed things around a bit to suit her own taste, it would feel more homey. Up till now, all she'd done was scrub and scrub and scrub some more. Although Hazard had obviously made an effort to clean the floors, the toilet and kitchen surfaces, she didn't feel right until she'd dug into every corner of every cupboard and closet. That would take some time, but the house had to smell fresh and clean for her to feel satisfied.

Tina and Christopher took turns having a quick shower and then dressed for dinner. She even put on earrings and slipped on high-heeled sandals to go with her sleeveless floral print dress.

Hazard drove into the yard to pick them up and whistled when he saw her come out. "You're looking pretty! I feel I should take you somewhere more fancy than Harold's." He opened the truck door for her and bowed. "Too bad there's nothing fancier at the rez. But since Harold's has the best food anywhere this side of heaven, I think we're good."

Tina climbed into the truck and sat down beside him. She hadn't minded the wolf whistle because it told her all her preparations had been noted and were appreciated. "Harold's will do just fine, thanks! Wherever there's food that I don't have to cook myself is great."

Christopher scampered up into the back seat and had some trouble buckling himself in with one hand. "My Mommy's pretty when she gets dressed up," he said. "Isn't she?"

"Your mommy's pretty even when she's not dressed up," Hazard said.

"Well, not that pretty."

Embarrassed, Tina reached back to give Christopher a slap on the arm. "Cut that out, both of you."

Harold's Diner was a small establishment with long fluorescent lights hanging from the ceiling. Tina couldn't help noting they were liberally speckled with fly droppings. There was an open kitchen on one side and about a dozen booths, tonight almost filled with diners. Near the entrance was the cash register, where a rather pretty woman was writing up a bill.

She smiled at Hazard exposing a missing side tooth. "Welcome, Chief," she said. "How was fishing at Beaver Lake?"

"Good," Hazard said. "I've got four trout in my freezer and I smoked a few."

"Didn't bring me none!" the woman grumbled, pouting.

"Tomorrow," Hazard promised. He turned to Tina who had come up beside him. "This is Shirley, a classmate of mine from way back. She's the best waitress on the rez. This lady here is the new teacher, Christina Lawrence."

Shirley gave Tina a shy smile. "Nice to meet you, Mrs. Lawrence. And this must be Christopher, eh? I've heard about you." She reached out to give him a pat on the head, which sent him shrinking back against his mother's side.

Tina was mortified and made a mental note to have a talk with Christopher about the proper way to greet people. She was absolutely certain he hadn't been like this in Toronto. Was it just that he didn't feel at home among these people? Toronto was about the most multicultural city in the world and meeting people of different races was a daily occurrence, even for Christopher, who lived in an area that was mostly white. So what was his problem?

But his rude manners didn't seem to bother Shirley, who only smiled. "I heard from James and Chogan that you got yourself a dog. That right, eh?"

"Yes. Hazard let me borrow Mutt while I'm living here," Christopher said, more at ease now that the dog had been mentioned. "But I'm taking Mutt to Toronto with me when we go back." He gave Hazard a sideways glance, as though challenging him, and then glared at his mother defiantly.

"You are?" Hazard and Tina asked in a chorus, and broke into a laugh.

"Yes, I am," Christopher said with so much determination in his voice that Tina's eyes blurred. She knew he had his little fingers crossed in the pocket of his jeans but was headed for a huge disappointment. No way was the dog coming to Toronto with them.

"Just seat yourselves," Shirley said, and as soon as they had found a booth, another woman came over to greet them.

"Well, aren't we privileged tonight," Hazard said with a grin. "This is Ms Anna herself, taking the time from her busy kitchen to come and say hello."

"I just wanted meet the new teacher," Anna said. She was a short, plump woman with a friendly smile and her black hair was tied back in a bun. "How are you Mrs. Lawrence? And Christopher?"

"I'm fine," Tina said getting up to shake Anna's hand. "Please call me Tina. Christopher, say hello to the lady."

"Hello to the lady," he mimicked.

Tina wanted to give him a swat on the behind, but lucky for him, he was sitting down. He was not usually a rude boy, but seemed to have totally lost his manners. And here they'd been away from home hardly more than a week.

"Anna's the wife of Harold. They own this place. Anna's absolutely the best pie maker north of Toronto," Hazard said.

"Oh, pooh! You stop that, Mr. Big Chief," Anna said with a laugh and tapped his shoulder with the menus she had with her. She turned to Tina. "My sister, Florence, lives just up the road from you. She's the mother of James and Chogan and she's been waiting to meet you."

"Oh, it will be very nice to get to know some of my neighbours," Tina said. So this Florence was expecting her to make the first move? Okay. She could do that.

Anna pulled out a rag from her apron pocket and wiped the crumbs off the table before handing them their menus. "It's been so busy this afternoon, Shirley hasn't got around to setting this table yet. Sorry 'bout that."

Before they'd even had a chance to look at the menus, Hazard said, addressing Christopher, "The pork chops and mashed potatoes here are totally wicked."

And since even Christopher liked pork chops, that's what they all decided on. Anna took their orders to the kitchen.

Tina would have liked to have a glass of wine with her meal but didn't dare to chance it, not knowing which brands were available out here. She was afraid to ask for some of her favourites because if they didn't carry them, she might have sounded snobbish. Just ordering the house red seemed a bit risky, so she opted instead to wait till she got home. There she had several bottles of her favourite Shiraz waiting.

Maybe she could even invite Hazard over for a glass? Or should she? Would that seem too much like she was looking for male company? Well, it would be nice to have him over for the evening. And maybe even for the night. Good lord! Where did that idea come from? Quickly and forcefully she squashed down the thought.

She concentrated on her pork chops, and was gratified to see Christopher clean off his plate right down to the last buttered carrot slice. At Hazard's urging, they ordered blueberry pie for dessert. It was so delicious that when he was done, Christopher licked his plate. Tina didn't even reprimand him and only wished she dared do likewise.

"I don't think I've tasted such flaky, tender crust

ever in my life!" she said and was glad she hadn't worn her skin-tight jeans. She would've had to pop open the top button, right in front of Hazard. "Christopher and I just might become regulars here and come for pie every day."

Hazard chuckled. "You wouldn't be the only ones, that's for sure. Anna's pies are world-famous. Okay, at least Greenstone-famous."

"They should be world-famous. In Toronto these pies would be jumping right off the bakery shelves so fast Anna wouldn't be able to keep up with the demand. She'd have to train an army of bakers to help her."

What a marvelous idea! Her marketing experience was now making her mind buzz with all the possibilities this could open up for Anna and her bakery-restaurant.

As she drank her coffee, Tina continued to struggle with the thought of inviting Hazard to come over for a glass of wine. What if he got the wrong message? What the hell! She might as well just bite the bullet and then deal with any misconceptions, if they came up. Maybe she could casually invite him when he dropped off her and Christopher, as though she'd just suddenly thought of the idea.

It was still light when the truck pulled up in front of her house. Christopher jumped out and ran to greet Mutt, whose tail wagged furiously at the sight of him.

Tina was half-way down off the truck, when she turned to Hazard and said brightly, "Hey, you want to come in for a glass of wine? I'd like to thank you for the dinner tonight." Did that sound like an impromptu invitation?

Hazard didn't take a second to consider the offer. He cut the motor and hopped out. "I was hoping you'd ask," he said, coming around to her side. "I was thinking it mightn't be proper for me to invite you to my house for a drink, but for me to visit you is okay. Right?"

"Right." Tina suppressed a giggle. Here they'd both been thinking about the same thing.

"Hazard is coming in for a while," she called to Christopher. "You make sure you stay in the yard where I can see you."

"I will," the boy shouted back."I just want to play with Mutt for a while. He missed me."

"Shall we make ourselves comfortable?" Tina indicated the kitchen table and chairs. She hoped sitting informally in the kitchen was less like "visiting for the evening" and more like "just dropping by".

She uncorked a bottle of red that she'd brought with her from Toronto and poured it into two tall beer mugs. She hadn't located any wine glasses in the house, but there were enough beer mugs to fill a whole shelf. Perhaps the previous occupant had had friends over for a few beers now and then.

"Wine from a beer mug," she said as she handed it to him. "I'm starting a new trend."

Hazard read the label on the bottle. "Not too shabby."

"It's my favourite, so I brought some with me, in case it's not locally available. I figured beer would more than likely be the drink of choice around here, being Northern Ontario."

"You figured that right." He raised his mug. "Here's to . . . what should we drink to?"

"To friendship?" Tina suggested.

"Sounds good to me. To friendship."

"And the next one can be to my new car," she said. "And the next one to my new job."

Hazard chuckled, shaking his head. "If we keep that up, I'll have to leave my truck here for the night."

Tina clapped a hand to her mouth. "Oh Lord! I forgot about that. When I have company I always have more than one glass of wine. You should have said no to my invitation."

"You think I'm crazy? I get invited to the home of a lovely lady for some wine and I should refuse? Not in this lifetime."

His words, spoken in his deep, full voice set off a tiny cyclone inside her. She lowered her gaze to pick at a loose thread from the cushion on the chair next to her.

"Well, it's true," Hazard said. "It's really nice to have you in Greenstone. You're the prettiest thing that's come here since . . . since forever."

That didn't help one bit, because now Tina felt the heat rise to her cheeks. Was he flattering her in hopes of starting something between them? Well, she definitely was not into starting anything, not even if this man sitting in front of her was as handsome as the Devil incarnated. Which he was.

"Aw . . . you're just saying that because it's true," she quipped to hide her discomfort.

Hazard laughed. "Not just pretty, but with a sense of humour, too. And by the way, you don't need to worry about me having too much wine, because I can always walk home if necessary."

"And leave your truck in my yard so everyone will

think you stayed the night? No way!" But the idea of him staying the night made her pulse kick up a notch and the heat rose to her cheeks again, making her pick at the chair cushion again. If she kept this up he would soon start to wonder why she was so intent on destroying a perfectly good cushion. Perfectly good, except for those mallards.

But she had to admit that under different circumstances, she wouldn't have minded a nocturnal visit from him. Too bad these were not the circumstances. She needed to lead the conversation off to something more neutral.

Just then Christopher rushed in. "I gotta pee!" he shouted, making a bee line for the bathroom.

"I've told you not to leave that to the last minute!" Tina cried after him as the bathroom door slammed shut. She shook her head. "He's always like that."

"He should learn to go against a tree like all little boys do," Hazard suggested.

"Yes, you already told him about that once, thank you very much. But that's not going to happen."

"Because . . .?"

She liked the way he cocked his head to one side when he asked that, almost quizzically.

"Because when we go home, I don't want him peeing against trees in Toronto's public parks. That's why not."

Hazard snorted. "I trust he's bright enough to know the difference between a natural forest and a public park."

Tina didn't want to continue this subject, but it suddenly reminded her of the outhouses at the school. She leaned her elbows on the table and looked at him earnestly. "But speaking of peeing, I would like to draw your attention once again to the outhouses."

"Yes?" He sounded cautiously defensive, like he wasn't sure where this was leading.

"They're very smelly."

"I realize that."

"So I guess there's no way the school could have indoor flush toilets?" She leaned back in her chair and continued to look him directly in the eye.

"No way. Each portable would have to have plumbing and water piped in. Right now there's water and a toilet only in the teacher's portable. And a much bigger septic bed would have to be dug. That would be much too expensive."

"Yes. I can see that," Tina said, but from the hesitation in her voice Hazard could tell she wasn't through.

"What?" he asked, and also sat back, getting ready to hear whatever was on her mind. She looked so rosy and fresh in her flowery dress it was difficult to keep his mind on the school's outhouses.

"I didn't say anything," Tina said with such a look of innocence on her pretty face that he knew something insidious was cooking in her brain.

"But you're thinking something. Let's hear it."

"How about composting toilets?" She again leaned forward enthusiastically. "I'm sure you've heard of them."

Christopher dashed past them without a word and the screen door slammed behind him.

"Of course I have. But they're way out of our snack bracket."

Hazard hated to shoot down her idea, but he'd recently

looked into a composting toilet for his own house, and found them to be too much for his budget.

"Not if you got a loan." Obviously she wasn't one to give up easily. "A long-term loan that could be paid back in small enough installments."

"You don't understand," Hazard tried to say as gently as he could. She was fired up with such enthusiasm he didn't want to see the sparkle die in her eyes as a result of his words. But facts were facts. "Where would this band get someone to loan us that kind of money?" He spread out his hands on the table, empty palms up.

But the sparkle in her eyes didn't die. "From me," she stated simply and grinned at him as though she'd solved the problem. "Bingo!" She got up to pour them each more wine.

Hazard groaned and shook his head. The woman was impossible. "I know you're not exactly poor," he began. "But that would be—"

"A great investment!" She began to circle the table in her enthusiasm, taking sips from her glass as she walked. "Composting toilets don't need water, and nowadays they're easy to operate and maintain. And as a bonus, they produce lovely compost that can be used in a garden in the school yard where the students can grow lettuce and tomatoes and carrots and radishes." She counted off each item on her fingers and finished by holding up both arms in victory. "Voilà!"

"But—" Hazard began but again Tina cut him off. She stopped behind him and put her hands on the back of his chair. Funny how he could feel her fingers even though she wasn't even touching him.

"But what?" she challenged. "There are no butts. This is a win-win situation all around. The only thing we'd need is a new, heated outhouse with electricity and . . . let's see . . . four stalls for the toilets."

"Four?"

"Two for girls, two for boys," Tina said cheerfully and started her circulating again. "The manpower to build the outhouse can come from the people at the reserve. Right?"

"And voilà?"

"Oui. Voilà!"

Hazard couldn't think of anything to say. This plan had to be unrealistic, but she made it sound so simple. Of course the fact that she was loaded probably made her think anything was possible.

He let his breath out in a long puff. "Now that we've solved the school's toilet problem, what's the next issue we can tackle?" He was joking, of course, but Tina stopped in front of him, her face beaming. It seemed her enthusiasm had no bounds.

"I'm glad you asked. Remember when I said I'd love to learn to bake pies like Anna's. Well, here's what I was thinking."

"Oh, oh," Hazard grimaced. Another harebrained idea coming up. "Sorry I asked."

"I thought I could pay her for the lessons and with that money she could pay for Shirley to get herself the tooth she's missing. Implants are expensive and dental insurance—if she has one—doesn't usually cover them."

Hazard frowned. Here she was again, trying to fix things at the rez that didn't need fixing. "I really don't think Shirley's too concerned about her missing tooth," he said. Tina was getting too close to poking her nose into the people's lives. He'd been afraid that she might be another do-gooder pushing her own ideas about personal hygiene and cleanliness, and that didn't sit well with him.

"Getting toilets for the school is one thing," he said. "But poking your nose into someone else's mouth is something totally different."

Tina stopped her pacing and looked at him, puzzled. "But every woman likes to have a nice smile," she said. "I'm sure Shirley would like it if that gap didn't show."

"You don't know that."

Tina sat down, the sparkle gone from her eyes and Hazard could have kicked himself for killing it.

They sipped their wine in downcast silence.

"I guess I should get going," Hazard said at last. "I'm okay to drive home, although I'd hate to have the RCMP stop me and charge me with being over the limit. That would shoot down my new program about Designated Drivers before it's even off the ground."

"I think you better leave the truck here and walk home," Tina said. "I was just joking about what people might say. I'm sure no one would even notice."

Hazard wasn't so sure about that, but nodded. "You're right. I'll do that. And since I don't have to worry about driving, I might as well agree to another—"

Furious barking from the backyard followed by loud yells from Christopher had them both jumping up simultaneously. Hazard knocked over his chair as he ran to the back door and flung it open. He was just in time to see a gray tail disappear into the bush.

Chapter Five

Tina tried to look over Hazard's broad shoulders as they both rushed out into the backyard. Mutt kept barking furiously and the hair on the back of his neck bristled. Christopher stood beside him, ramrod straight, hands high in the air.

She heard Hazard murmur, "Don't you dare say it was Mutt's doing. Tell him how brave he was to scare the coyote away."

"C-coyote?" Tina stammered. "That was a coyote?" Her legs turned to jelly and dizzying circles swam in her head. She gripped Hazard's arm for support to prevent herself from fainting.

"Look! I scared it away!" Christopher shouted. "I did just like you told me, Hazard. I didn't turn away and I made myself look big and I waved my arms high in the air. It worked!"

"Now buck up." Hazard whispered to Tina and gently removed her arm. He went over to Christopher, slapped the boy on the shoulder and said, "Well done, buddy. You were great!"

"Well, Mutt helped, too," Christopher admitted with a modest shrug. "But I did just what you told me and it worked." His face glowed with pride like Tina had never seen before.

She stepped up and stroked Mutt's head. The dog was beginning to settle down after the excitement. "Good dog," she whispered. "Thank you." Then she went to Christopher and patted him on the shoulder. She wanted to hug him and squeeze him hard against her, but instead she croaked out, "You were very brave, honey."

"Shouldn't call me honey, Mommy." Christopher said. "You should call me brave."

"I just did."

"I mean Indian Brave. Like Hazard." He turned adoring eyes up to Hazard.

Once again, despite the maelstrom of emotions tumbling through her—alarm, fear, and relief at her son's safety—Tina couldn't prevent feeling a stab of resentment from sneaking into her heart. Christopher was looking to Hazard for everything that had previously been her job to provide. She was the one who'd always provided praise, advice and encouragement. It was like her status in Christopher's life was slipping away. Irritation made her say exactly what Hazard had told her not to say. "Well, I think it was mainly Mutt's barking and growling that scared the coyote away," she blurted out.

She could feel Hazard's eyes pierce right through her, and looked up to see him scowling. Christopher's enthusiasm dimmed before her eyes.

"I . . . I did what Hazard taught me," he stammered, looking from one to the other. "Didn't I, Hazard? And it worked. Right?"

"It sure did," Hazard said. "If you hadn't waved your

arms the coyote might have attacked Mutt and hurt him."

Christopher's face beamed again. "Yeah, that's what I figgered. I didn't want them to get into a fight." He went over to Mutt and, with his good hand, scratched behind his ears. "You probably would've beat him anyway, boy, but you might have got a cut and then we'd have to take you to the vet and get you stitched and bandaged like me."

He turned to Hazard, sudden concern on his face. "Where's the vet? I need to know in case Mutt gets hurt."

"Well, there's no vet in town," Hazard told him. "But in Spruce Falls there's a man who knows a lot about animals."

Enough of this camaraderie. The irritation still burned inside Tina. Or was it jealousy? "Let's get inside, Christopher," she said briskly. "It's past nine and you need to be in bed soon."

"Aw, Mommy, it's still daylight," the boy whined. "And summer holidays."

"Stop whining, Christopher," she snapped. "I'm tired of your whining. Say good night to Hazard and Mutt and get inside like I said."

She knew without looking that there would be disapproval in Hazard's black eyes. She would have disapproved, too, if she could have looked at herself. What was the matter with her, anyway?

Christopher slipped his arms around Hazard's waist and hugged him. "Good night, Hazard," he said and then turned to hug the dog. "Good night, Mutt."

As he walked into the house, his shoulders slumped, and Tina felt like she'd just killed a butterfly.

The joy and pride on her son's face, when he'd scared off the coyote, was gone.

Hazard didn't say anything, but Tina raised both hand, palms toward him. "I know, I know, I know. I don't know what came over me. I'm so embarrassed. Such behavior! I'm so very sorry."

"There's no need to be embarrassed, Tina," Hazard said it so gently, that her eyes filled with tears. "You've just had a huge scare and you're upset. It's natural to act out."

"But I'm an adult," Tina protested, the tears now welling out. "I'm not supposed to act out! That's for kids."

Hazard took her face between his hands and forced her to look up at him. "Sometimes it's okay for adults to act out like kids." He chuckled. "Like when you were so excited about the composting toilet idea that you kept circling the table and waving your arms."

Tina stepped back. His touch produced more turmoil inside her, and it was more emotion than she could handle right now. "I guess I did," she admitted, turning to go in. "But those toilets must not just stay an idea. I want to make them a reality."

"Hey, Hazard!" It was Tina on the phone. The clock radio on his night table was about to wake him up with the six o'clock morning news, but Tina beat CBC to it.

Hazard rubbed his eyes and croaked, "Good morning. What's going on?"

"My dad is into making small loans to people who are good for paying back. I called him and he agrees it's a good investment."

"What is?" What the hell was she so excited about?

He shut off the radio that was trying to shock him awake with news of another terrorist attack.

"The composting toilets, of course! Dad will loan the money."

The woman was crazy. "They're not a good investment," Hazard said."They won't increase in value. They're like a car."

"But it's an investment in the health and well-being of the children," she insisted. "So if you can get the men to build a new outhouse . . . Does anyone know how to install electricity?"

It was no use fighting it. He was compelled to answer. "Yeah, Joe Wind Song does. He took a course in Big Thunder a few years ago."

"Well, could you talk to him and ask him if he has time to do the wiring?"

Little by little her enthusiasm grabbed him along, despite his brain trying to convince him this was a dumb idea. Composting toilets, for God's sake! "Okay, I'll do that."

"Today?"

The woman certainly wasted no time. "Yes, today."

"Good." It sounded like the matter was settled, but then she went on. "And the lumber for the new outhouse? I don't want to use any of that smelly stuff from the old outhouse. That's got to be burned."

"Burned. Right."

"Where does one get lumber around here?"

"Spruce Falls is the closest place. They have a lumber mill." It was so easy to get carried along on the current of her enthusiasm that Hazard found himself getting slightly excited about the project. He put the phone on speaker while he pulled on his jeans and zipped them up.

"Good. I assume there's someone on the rez who knows how to order all the wood? Two-by-sixes for the floor joists, two-by-fours for the wall studs, and all that?"

"Excuse me, but how is it you know so much about lumber and electricity? I thought you were a rich city girl."

Her laughter bubbled over the phone. "I'm just interested in things. I watched them build a shed at the cottage and asked a lot of questions. And on the internet there are instructions for just about anything one wants to construct."

"Yes, but—"

"But, but, but," Tina's laughing voice over the phone told him she was joking. "There'll always be buts. You just have to get over them. Buck up, as you said to me."

"Right. Now do you mind if I put the coffee on and get ready for work? This hare-brained plan of yours is going to waste some of my office time today."

"And don't forget you said you would come and unstick the portable windows on your lunch hour," she caroled before hanging up.

What a whirlwind! Obviously when she got something in her mind, she didn't wait a minute to get things rolling.

"Christopher, I want you to go through all those papers and stack them neatly on the floor," Tina said. They were in the portable with the door open for airing. The day was sunny and warm, and a soft breeze breathed into the room from time to time. After she had washed the worn linoleum flooring with a cleaning solution the previous day, the room didn't smell quite as bad. But she would have been happier if she'd been able to rip off the linoleum and check for mold between it and the wooden floor. It couldn't be good.

Tina tossed an empty cardboard box on the floor in front of Christopher. "Make one pile for lined paper, one for blank paper, and then all the coloured construction paper can go into this box. Got it?"

"Yeah, got it."

She had bribed Christopher with money toward a new collar and leash for Mutt. And maybe even a heavy stainless steel water dish that wouldn't fly away in a strong breeze, like the plastic one had a way of doing.

By noon Christopher was beginning to whine, ready to call it a day, while Tina was still roaring to go. She had emptied the two closets and thrown away sundry items that the previous teacher had left behind. Obviously a man, judging from the broken electric shaver she found.

In the afternoon she planned to start working on the bulletin board on the wall opposite the windows. She wanted to cover it with a cheerful yellow paper, and staple on a colourful alphabet and funny pictures of numbers. The kids could then draw portraits of themselves with their names to pin on it.

"Hello, are you taking new pupils?" Hazard peeked in through the open door.

"I am, but you have to be at least five years old," Tina quipped. "Though your large size is a bit deceiving, you might fit the bill."

Christopher laughed uproariously at the joke as he ran up to give Hazard a hug. Hazard put the paper coffee cup he was carrying on the window ledge and lifted the boy up, throwing him high in the air.

Tina looked on with a mixture of joy and dread. If Christopher became too fond of Hazard, the parting, when it came, could be painful.

"Brought you coffee from Harold's," Hazard said and handed Tina the cup.

"Thanks." Gratefully she took a sip while Hazard used a hammer and a crowbar, to get the windows unstuck. Soon more fresh, clean air streamed into the room.

"Do you want to join us for some lunch, as a reward for your efforts?" Tina asked him.

"I'd like that very much." Hazard sat down on one of the tiny primary chairs. He couldn't get his knees under the desk and had to sit sideways. "What are we serving?"

"You can help yourself to a salmon salad sandwich. This coffee is much appreciated, thank you, because I've already finished what I brought with me in the thermos."

"I'm going outside to eat," Christopher announced. "Mutt is lonely."

Tina couldn't remember Christopher ever being outside on his own when they lived in Toronto, and she found it difficult to get used to him being out of sight.

"We could all go out and eat in the sunshine, rather than sit inside this musty classroom," she suggested. "Although it's a lot better now with the fresh air flowing in."

Tina collected up the sandwiches and carried them out onto the portable steps. "But speaking of musty," she began as soon as she was seated. "I don't suppose

I'm allowed to have someone rip up that linoleum flooring and wash the wood underneath with a disinfectant?" Didn't hurt to ask, she always figured. The
worst he could do was decline her request. "We could
then lay on new linoleum."

"Well, that would cost . . ." Hazard hesitated as he
bit into a sandwich, but since he didn't immediately
shoot down the idea, Tina sensed a possible victory.

"How much?" she asked eagerly.

"Of course we would have to do it for both portables. It wouldn't be fair to just renew your floor. Right?
That could cost plenty. Good sandwich, by the way."

Tina suspected he wanted to change the subject.
"Okay, let's leave the floors for now, although linoleum
is not expensive." She didn't want to push any more
new ideas that could ruin her plans for the composting
toilets. "The toilets can be the big expense for this year.
Maybe the floors can be on next year's budget."

Next year's budget? Why was she thinking of next
year when she wouldn't even be here? Of course there
was no reason the linoleum couldn't be laid on the
classroom floors even if she was out of the picture. She
was just throwing the idea out for consideration.

But sure enough, Hazard caught it. "So, you're
planning to be around next year to lay the linoleum on
the floors?"

"That's not what I said," Tina countered. "I simply
said it can be an item on next year's budget."

"Right."

She thought she could hear disappointment in the
word. That puzzled her, because did it make any difference whether it was she or another teacher enjoying
the new linoleum?

They ate in silence and watched Christopher run around the yard with Mutt.

"So you're ready to drive to Big Thunder this Saturday?" Hazard asked and crumpled up the sandwich paper in one big hand. "I assume you've found out where there's an SUV dealer in town."

"Of course," Tina replied and began to pack away the leftovers. "I called them and told them I'm coming. They'll have a car ready when we get there. A deep red colour."

Hazard gave a long whistle. "Holy mackerel, woman! You really don't waste time, do you?" He got up, stretched his lanky frame and followed Tina inside.

"No, I don't. You recommended an SUV. I looked at them online and decided you're right. It seems like just the vehicle for me, so that's what I'm getting." She stuffed the plastic sandwich containers into a cloth bag.

"Period. End of story," Hazard said with a laugh. "You are one incredible package of energy, you know that?" He placed his hands on her shoulders, and gave her a playful shake. "Don't you ever rest?"

She liked his touch. It was okay to feel good—just for a while—with his hands touching her, making electric sparks flow through her body. It was a feeling she hadn't enjoyed since . . . forever.

"Back to work," she said briskly and moved away. His hands fell to his sides as he released her, making her feel she'd just lost something very wonderful. But she brushed the feeling aside with a shrug. Not having had a date for so long would make any woman appreciate the feel of a man's hands on her.

In a blur of activity Tina prepared her classroom for the opening day of school. As it loomed closer and closer, her nervous-index rose exponentially. Would she really be able to teach all these kids whose cultural background was so different from hers? Would she be able to accept their different home-life—not to mention personal hygiene, especially where they came in contact with Christopher? The boy's hand was healing well and one day when the doctor was at the clinic they had gone to show it to him. He had removed the sutures, but now Tina was even more vigilant about Christopher's hygiene and kept reminding him to keep his hands clean.

One day, while Tina and Christopher were working in the classroom, her fellow teacher and school principal finally showed up. He peeked in, after tapping on the door which Tina still kept open to rid the room of any lingering musty odours.

"Hi, I'm Steve Miller, the principal," the man said and stepped in. "I brought your class list and attendance book and other 'important' papers." He did the air-quotes as he said that, as though he were dismissing the papers as trivial, and marched past her to deposit them on her desk.

"I'm Christina Lawrence." She extended her hand, which he took in his and held just long enough to make it obvious he was extending the handshake on purpose. Tina was of two minds whether to yank her hand away, but decided to play nice. It wouldn't do to start this relationship on a negative note.

Steve sat down on the only adult chair in the room and yawned. "Just got back from the 'big city'." Air-quotes again. "Big Thunder. As you know, I 'teach' (air-quotes) the junior and intermediate classes. And I use the word teach loosely."

Yes, she'd noticed. Tina hopped up to sit on the teacher's desk.

"I see." She wasn't sure what it was about him that turned her off. The extended handshake? The liberal use of air-quotes? Or the way he made his teaching sound trivial and unimportant. She made an effort to dismiss such feelings. He was probably a very nice person once she got to know him.

"Have you heard that I spoke with Hazard about composting toilets?" Tina began eagerly. "I think I've convinced him that they beat outhouses in every respect."

Steve's response was less than favourable. "They'll get wrecked," he said airily. "The kids will vandalize them, and someone is bound to come and steal them. These people steal everything that's not nailed down."

Her impression of Steve took a huge plunge.

She squinted at him. "That so?"

He wasn't a bad-looking fellow. Blond, fairly tall, and around fortyish, but as far as she was concerned, that was the end of his attributes. His attitude stank.

"I've taught here for two years and this one's gonna be my last," Steve then told her.

At this point, Tina couldn't have cared less. She made a sound that could have meant anything.

"Yeah, I'm going back home and find myself a wife," he said with a suggestive wink that was too lecherous for her liking. "Been lonely here long enough."

Tina wasn't the least bit interested in his loneliness. Something about him made her feel this man was not above taking advantage of whatever comforts he could.

"You want the job of principal when I leave?" he asked. "We could advertise for a new one, or you could just take over."

"I don't have my principal's qualifications," Tina said.

Steve snorted disdainfully. "Qualifications? Who needs qualifications? I'm not qualified, but they couldn't get anyone else, so here I am, getting paid for being a principal and a teacher. Not bad, eh?"

His laughter grated her ears.

"Indeed." Tina squirmed uncomfortably on the table. What would it be like teaching next door to a man who seemed to lack principles? She could only hope, since her pupils were so much younger than his, that she wouldn't need to be involved too much with him. Since he was her principal she probably wouldn't be able to avoid him totally, but she'd already made up her mind to eat her lunch in her own classroom, rather than in the separate teachers' portable.

Steve looked out to where Christopher was running around with Mutt. "That your son?"

"Yes. That's Christopher. He's going to grade one."

So, where's his father? Steve's expression seemed to be asking, but thank the Lord he didn't voice the question or she would promptly have walked him to the door and told him to mind his own business. Obviously the man at least had a modicum of couth.

Tina hopped off the desk. "It's time I got back to work."

Luckily Steve rose without being invited out. "You're doing such a great job with your room. I'll have to have you fix up mine, too."

She forced out a laugh. "No thanks. Getting this portable cleaned was enough of a chore for me. You'll have to do your own dirty work."

"Oh, I'll just get a couple of the women to come and clean it," he said casually. "That's what you should have done, too."

"Well, since no one informed me about such services, I did it myself." She was going to point out that, as the principal, Steve could have told her about the janitorial arrangements in their scant communications.

After he left, Tina didn't feel much like working any more, so she told Christopher they would walk to the Hudson's Bay store where he could choose himself a treat.

"You can buy the dog collar and food dish in Big Thunder. I'm sure there's a better selection at one of the bigger stores."

Chapter Six

Tina was happy that, with Mutt as the intermediary, Christopher had become good friends with James and Chogan. The brothers came over often, eager to play with the toys and electronic gadgets Christopher had brought with him from Toronto. And whenever the weather permitted, he played with Mutt and the brothers outside. But the most wonderful thing about this new friendship was, that Christopher had finally stopped whining.

For the long drive to Big Thunder, Tina had asked the brothers if they would like to come along to keep Christopher company. The brothers had, very shyly, said they would, and Florence, their mother, was agreeable.

Tina had met Florence when she had walked over to ask if there was a hairdresser in town. She'd used that an excuse to go and visit her neighbour, after finding out that Florence was expecting her to make the first move. Florence was friendly but very shy, which explained why she hadn't dropped in with a casserole or warm cookies to welcome them, as Tina had first expected.

Florence had told her that Yvette was the town's hairdresser, a French-Canadian woman who worked at home in her spare bedroom. Her husband, Joe Wind Song, was the electrician Hazard had mentioned earlier.

The three boys were now sitting in the back seat of the truck playing computer games. James and Chogan talked quietly, but Christopher's voice sometimes filled the whole interior, especially when he broke into an outburst of laughter. Tina didn't mind seeing her son so happy for it had the same effect on her.

They drove along the highway, through the rough and peaceful Northern Ontario, dotted with sparkling lakes and rushing rivers. Tina and Hazard were having a nice conversation which rather surprised her. For a First Nations man she thought Hazard was quite talkative, breaking the Hollywood stereotype she had of a "strong, silent Indian". She liked to listen to his low, soft voice telling her about life on the Greenstone Reserve, and about the activities the people engaged in. She was surprised to hear almost everyone—women and men, the young and the old—regularly went fishing to supplement their diet or just for fun, and many still engaged in trapping and hunting.

"My cousin, Leah, is an avid hunter and every fall she shoots her quota of deer," Hazard told her. "The odd moose, too. She's quite the marksman, or markswoman, I guess I should say."

"I don't think I'd have the heart to shoot an animal."

"Yeah, you probably couldn't do it," Hazard said. "But Leah makes good use of the meat. She has three kids and feeds them mainly on the deer meat plus the fish they catch."

"Our mom traps rabbits," James said from the back seat.

"What? She kills little bunnies?" Christopher cried, horrified. "That's not nice."

"Rabbit stew is good," said Chogan. "You can come and have some next time Mom makes it."

"No, thank you!"

Christopher's firm reply put a definite end to that line of conversation.

"We haven't never been to Big Thunder," Tina heard James tell Christopher.

"Yeah," Chogan agreed. "I wanna see the big sky-scrapers 'n' everythin'."

"When we were waiting for the bus in Big Thunder, I didn't see any—" Christopher began but was inter-rupted by Hazard.

"There sure are some pretty tall buildings in Big Thunder. Twelve stories, even."

"That's not a—" Christopher tried again.

Again Hazard interrupted. "It's like they scrape the sky. Especially when they're high up on a hill."

Tina understood Hazard didn't want to spoil the boys' excitement about their first visit to the big city and she went along. "They're big, all right. And they have lots of car dealers. We'll go pick up my car right after lunch. They should have it ready to go."

"The beauty of internet," Hazard said.

They reached Big Thunder four hours later.

"Lunch time!" Tina announced as the boys tumbled out of the truck in front of a small diner.

The boys and Hazard ordered the usual burgers and fries, while Tina settled on a chicken salad. After finishing off with ice cream sundaes, the boys scrambled back into the truck and James and Chogan craned their necks to see the tall buildings, the traffic lights, and the store display windows.

"Hey, Christopher, maybe we should go and pick up that fishing tackle for you I was talking about earlier," Hazard said. "Would you like that?"

"Yes, thank you." Christopher's reply was polite and lacked enthusiasm.

Tina felt sorry for Hazard who couldn't get a more excited response, but with Christopher's lack of experience with fishing, that was to be expected.

"Remember the whoppers Hazard told you about?" she reminded Christopher.

That worked.

"Yes!" the boy now shouted. "We'll catch those whoppers!"

Tina knew it was just the sound of the word that brought on this change, because he had no idea what a "whopper" was. But soon he would be able to experience the real excitement of catching one with Hazard.

Yes, Hazard again. He was becoming very important in all matters having to do with their life. Too important.

They entered a large mall that had a sporting goods store. Tina saw the eyes of James and Chogan grow big at the sight of the huge selection of fishing gear. Probably the reaction Hazard had hoped to get from Christopher.

"Wow! James breathed, his dark eyes shining. "Lookit all this stuff!"

Chogan walked off to circle the store and Tina

smiled as she watched him touch the shiny lures, rods and reels with longing fingers. She would definitely get something for the brothers because they couldn't possibly leave the store empty-handed.

"Hey! Indian boy! Keep your thieving fingers off the merchandise."

The shout made Chogan freeze in his tracks. Tina saw his big, frightened eyes look to her for help, and like an angry bee she rushed over.

She confronted the clerk, her eyes sparking with rage. "The boy is with me!" she pronounced, loudly enough for everyone around them to hear.

"Oh, sorry, lady," the clerk stammered.

"You don't owe me an apology," Tina said, "But you do owe one to this boy." She put a hand on Chogan's shoulder and stood in front of the clerk, daring him to refuse.

The clerk turned beet red, but finally coughed out a barely audible, "Sorry."

"Tell him you accept his apology," she said to Chogan, who squirmed uncomfortably under her hand. "Tell him he must not to do it again."

But the boy quickly backed away and ran to Hazard.

Tina again faced the clerk. "He forgives you, but from now on, please do not be rude to your customers. That's bad business."

Hazard and the boys resumed their inspection of the fishing gear while Tina followed behind, still shaking in anger from the encounter. Chogan, on the other hand, seemed to have recovered with no ill effects and was eagerly looking at everything.

Hazard picked out a shiny blue rod and reel, a

tackle box and some lures and handed them to Christopher. "How do these look?"

Christopher thanked him politely and held the gear awkwardly against his chest.

"So what would you boys like to have?" Tina asked James and Chogan, who gazed on Christopher's fancy gear with envious eyes.

The brothers didn't take long to make up their minds. Shyly they pointed to shiny red reels and rods.

Hazard came over to look at the price tags and surreptitiously shook his head. "Ouch," he whispered.

"Is it good quality?" Tina asked him.

He nodded. "Excellent."

Tina shrugged. What did she know about the price of fishing equipment? As long as it was quality stuff, that's all she needed to know. "Okay, then, we'll take them."

So while Hazard paid for Christopher's gear, she used her credit card to pay for what James and Chogan had chosen.

"Let's go pick up my car, now, before I run out of money!" Tina cried as they piled back into the truck.

The brothers looked at her in alarm.

"Oh, don't worry, I was just joking!" Tina said, laughing.

"My mommy never runs out of money," Christopher assured James and Chogan.

"Our mom runs out of money all the time," James said.

"No kidding? Then my mommy can give some to your mom. Can't you, Mommy?"

This was going into awkward territory. "Boys! Look at that funny moose," Tina cried pointing to a life-sized statue of the animal. "It's wearing a fancy flower hat." This distracted the kids and the conversation about money was forgotten.

At the car dealership everyone eagerly jumped out. Tina went inside to fill out the paperwork, while Hazard and the boys stayed outside. She smiled as she saw them all through the window circling the new cars and kicking a few tires.

When all the signing was done and the car paid for, Tina went out and followed the salesman to a sparkling deep red SUV. The man went through all the instructions, while Hazard kept eager Christopher from interrupting.

At last Tina turned to them and waved her keys high in the air. "Who wants to drive back home with me in the new car?" she called out. The three boys rushed to her side and they all laughed at the sad face Hazard pulled.

"I guess that shows who's the most popular one around here!" Tina crowed.

"I hate to disappoint you, but it's your car that's popular, not you," Hazard pointed out and then, out of the corner of his mouth, he muttered, "I'll enjoy the silent trip."

They set off, with Tina taking the lead in her dazzling new car. But no sooner had they reached the highway and started to coast along smoothly, when two deer ran out across the road in front of them. The animals missed the car, but the incident set her pulse into high gear.

"That was close!" she exclaimed.

But only a few seconds later, Hazard saw another deer spring out of the bush, obviously trying to catch up with the others. Though inside his truck, he heard the horrible crunch as the deer smashed into the SUV. The animal flew over the windshield, landing on the road in front of him, but he was able to swerve just in time and avoided hitting it.

Heart pounding, Hazard pulled to a stop. He jumped out and ran to Tina's car, where the hood stuck up skyward. He wrenched open the driver's door and his heart almost stopped. Tina sat, slumped over the steering wheel. The three boys in the back were obviously unhurt, because they all scrambled out and ran to look at the deer that was still feebly moving its legs.

"Tina!" Hazard croaked and gently touched her shoulder. "Tina! Say something!"

Relief flooded through him when she raised her head and looked at him, although her eyes were dazed. She was alive, but obviously had been banged by the exploding airbag.

"Oh, Lord," she moaned. "What a smash-up. My new car. I can't believe it."

He helped her out of the car. "Are you okay?" He asked, hardly able to get the words out in his concern.

Apparently she was, because no sooner was she out than she hurried to see the deer on the side of the road. It gave one more kick with its rear leg and then lay still.

"Oh, the poor thing," she moaned.

"I'm afraid it's gone," Hazard said to the boys who kept circling the animal with morbid interest.

Christopher pointed to the red pool that was slowly spreading on the road from under the deer's head. "Lookit all the blood!" He ran over to his mother who was leaning against the car. "See all the blood, Mom?"

"Yes, honey." Her voice sounded faint. "I did." She turned to Hazard. "I think I'm going to . . ." She buried her face in his shoulder.

Hazard wrapped his arms around her and held her against his chest as the after-effects of the accident started to set in. She trembled violently and her shoulders shook with dry sobs, while he murmured soothing words into her hair and stroked her back. He wanted to keep her there in his arms for the rest of the day. For the rest of your life, said a small voice inside him, but he squashed it down fiercely. Those kinds of thoughts had no place in this situation. She was in his arms only for comfort, but holding her there, it was difficult to make these errant thoughts disappear completely.

"Keep off the road, guys," Hazard called to the boys, who buzzed like bees around the carcass and paid no attention to the traffic. Several cars and pick-up trucks had already stopped on the side of the road and the people gathered around, some to gawk, and others to see if they could help.

"I have to call a tow truck and the police," Hazard said, reluctantly extricating Tina from his arms. "Are you okay here, or do you want to go sit in my truck?"

"I'm sorry I'm being such a baby but for some reason I c-can't seem to stop sh-shaking," she muttered. "I should be happy the boys weren't hurt and I shouldn't be like this. I'm so sorry. That poor animal."

"My darling, you've had a shock. That's a natural reaction, so just let it happen. It's nothing to apologize for." Hazard wished the d-word hadn't slipped out. But it had, and now he waited for a reaction. Which didn't come, thank God. She probably hadn't even heard it. He helped Tina into his truck where she sat leaning against the back rest, hugging herself.

Hazard dug out his phone and, after calling the police, he dialed the local tow truck number which someone in the crowd helpfully supplied to him.

"I think we'll be all right now," he said loudly over the cacophony of voices. "The tow truck and police will be here soon." The approaching sound of sirens could already be heard. "Better give the police room to do their thing."

Slowly the people got into their vehicles and drove off. A dead deer wasn't anything to write home about in these parts. By the time the police arrived a moment later, the roadside was almost clear.

But before the accident report had been made, the deer and the car towed away, the insurance company alerted, a new car ordered and Florence brought up to date on the situation, several hours had passed. It was dinner time, but Tina was in no mood to eat.

"You guys go ahead," she said to Hazard and the boys, "I'm going to just sit in the truck and have a nap. For some reason I feel a bit tired."

Concerned, Hazard looked at her. "Did you hit your head? Maybe you have a concussion."

"No, I didn't hit my head," Tina said. "And I have no bumps or sore spots anywhere. I think it was just the air bag that bumped me. Please stop worrying."

"I still think we should go to the hospital and have you checked out."

She laughed. "Honestly, I'm just tired. The boys aren't the least bit worried about me, so don't you be, either."

Hazard shrugged. "I know a bit more about these things than the boys do, so I have a right to worry."

"True enough," she said and climbed into the truck. "But I want you all to go and eat and leave me to have a nap."

Hazard took the boys to a pizza joint for the fastest possible meal. After wolfing down his slice, he waited impatiently for the kids to finish theirs. He didn't want to spoil their fun as they laughed and goofed around, stretching the cheese on their pizzas into long, dangling strings. Then they slurped the bottoms of their chocolate milk glasses with their straws, making the loudest possible noises. Normally this would have amused him, but now Hazard wanted to hurry back to make sure Tina was okay.

When they were back at the truck, Tina announced she wanted to arrange for a rental car, but Hazard wouldn't hear of it.

"Over my dead body are you going to drive all that distance back on your own after the accident," he countered vehemently.

"Honestly, Hazard, I'm perfectly okay now," she tried to reassure him. "Not even tired any more. And I don't even have a headache. I won't fall asleep at the wheel."

"Nevertheless, you're not driving,' Hazard said, firmly closing the debate. "We're all going back in the truck."

"But now someone will have to drive me back here to get my new vehicle," she tried one last protest.

"And someone will."

To his relief the stubborn woman saw it his way and agreed without further arguments.

They drove along the highway in the approaching evening twilight, and from time to time Hazard glanced at Tina, who sat beside him. She looked tired, and he hoped it was only from the shock of the accident and not from something physical, like a concussion. He also hoped she wasn't remembering the d-word that had escaped from his mouth. If she had heard it, he hoped she didn't read any meaning into it, because, honestly, there was none. It was the way he would have comforted and soothed any woman in that situation. Right?

Wrong. It was only her.

A week later Christopher was sitting at the kitchen table, eating an unusually early breakfast.

"What if I don't wanna to go fishing?" he muttered, reluctantly licking his porridge spoon. "There's mosquitoes and stuff. And fish are yucky and slimy and smelly."

Tina ignored the complaining. "Hazard will be here soon. Finish your porridge." She kept her voice matter-of-fact so he wouldn't think she was pressuring him—which she was, of course. It would do him good to learn to fish. And, more importantly, it would give her a chance to concentrate on her school work today without having to find things for him to do.

As Christopher was scraping the bottom of his bowl, Tina heard Hazard's truck drive up.

"Go get your jacket," she said to Christopher over her shoulder and went to answer the door. Hazard stood there and came in at her bidding. The handsome devil look about him never failed to send waves of pleasure through her. He'd been away on a hunting trip the previous week and since his return she'd seen him only once when he dropped by to see the progress in her classroom. This morning he looked particularly hazardous. His hair, usually combed off his forehead, now was tousled and the dark growth of beard made him appear rugged and dangerous. The jeans that hugged his thighs left not a single muscle to her imagination.

Tina swallowed. "You look like you're ready for an outdoor adventure," she commented when she was sure she could say the words without stammering.

"Scruffy, you mean?" Hazard grinned and swept the hair off his forehead. "I decided to leave shaving and showering till we get back, because I know I'll smell pretty strong after baiting hooks and cleaning fish all morning.

"Ugh!" Tina laughed and made a face.

"But them's the facts of fishing, you know."

"Yes, I guess a lot of things in life are pretty messy," she said, and then blushed. Like sex—full of smells and slick places.

Thank goodness he couldn't read her mind. She turned to snap the closures on Christopher's jacket strictly out of habit, but he soon told her what he though of that.

"Mommy, I can do them up myself. I'm not a baby," he complained. "And I don't need the jacket closed."

"It's only six o'clock," Hazard said. "The morning air's a bit cool. Better do it up."

And of course Christopher did exactly what Hazard suggested. Tina tried to keep the bitterness from invading her mind, but it annoyed her that this man was always able to maneuver her son to do his bidding, while she had to fight every step of the way whenever she asked him to do anything. It just didn't seem fair.

When Hazard and Christopher had left Tina walked over to the school. Today her plan was to finally wash the desks and chairs. Although there was no hot water, she could wash them outside by the water tap and let the wind and sun dry them. As soon as she unlocked her portable, she dragged the furniture outside and, using plenty of water, disinfectant soap and elbow grease, she scrubbed them clean, paying special attention to the grimy desk interiors.

She looked forward to checking out the storage room in the teachers' portable and getting some supplies. Ever since she was a little girl, the start of the school year had always excited her, with the pencils, crayons, erasers, and workbooks smelling fresh and new.

While the furniture was drying in the sunshine, she walked to the teachers' portable. Steve sat at the lunch table smoking a cigarette. Smoking inside? Another reason why she would not darken the door of this portable unless she had to.

"Hi. I decided to look around our staff room," she said lightly as she passed by him. Steve grunted in reply. She definitely did not like the fellow or his smoking, but it wouldn't be worth bringing this up. It could lead to a confrontation and she had decided it was better to swallow her dislike and keep the peace in this small school. Besides, she wasn't planning to be here for long. Maybe just till Christmas.

The portable was divided into three sections. One half was the lunch room with a counter, a sink, a stove and a small fridge, plus a long table and some chairs.

One door from it led to a bathroom with a sink and a toilet. Tina peeked in and crinkled her nose. No one had been to clean it all summer, judging from the smell.

Another door led to a small storage room where supplies were kept. Tina slipped in, closing the door behind her to prevent the cigarette smoke from entering the small enclosed space. On the long shelves that ran along one wall, she she started to look through the piles of workbooks for the ones she wanted. She picked out some with red and blue lines for printing practice, and some half-blank ones for stories and drawings. Her arms were full when she heard the door open, but didn't bother to turn, because it could only be Steve.

"I'll be out in a minute, if you don't mind waiting," she said, keeping her voice cordial. There wasn't room for two people to stand side-by-side in the narrow space.

"Hello, beautiful," Steve said in a low, mellifluous voice. Before she could react, he had his hands around her waist.

"Steve, that is not appropriate," Tina said severely in the tone she would have used when talking to an unruly student. "I don't appreciate you touching me."

But it soon became evident he was no unruly student, because his hands came up and around, slipping under the books to clamp her breasts.

With a flutter of pages the workbooks fell from her arms and scattered onto the floor as she whirled to face him. "Do not ever do that again," she spat out venomously. "If you even come close to me I will report you to the authorities."

Steve was obviously taken aback, but managed to

sneer, "They won't do anything. They get reports all the time from the women."

"All the time?" Tina's voice rose with sarcasm. "There are that many attacks on women here?"

"Sure. They ask for it," Steve scoffed.

"Sure they do, just like I asked for this, right?" She squeezed past him and held open the door of the storage room. "Get out, and don't ever come in while I'm in here."

"You don't own this place," Steve retorted.

His childish remark almost made Tina laugh out loud, but she didn't want him to misunderstand the seriousness of her words.

"I want to be able to work in peace with you until I leave. That means you don't come near me and never set foot in this room if I am in here. And never come into my classroom."

Steve slunk by her without a word.

"Is that clear?" Tina threw the question at his back. She wanted to be absolutely sure he understood she meant business.

"Yeah, yeah, yeah," he tossed over his shoulder and shuffled into the kitchen.

Rage shook her. What a reprehensible piece of garbage. She hoped this was the end of it because she had no desire to cause problems. But if he persisted, she wouldn't hesitate to report him and end his teaching career forever.

She didn't want to tell Hazard about this incident because Lord only knew what his reaction would be. As long as this was the end of Steve's lecherous behavior, then there was no need to create any bigger waves.

The desks were almost dry when she got back with

her arms full of supplies. She carried the furniture back into the portable and arranged them in rows. Kindergartens, grade ones, grade twos and threes. From her class list she knew how many desks should go in each row. Later, when she knew the kids and had her program running, she would see about arranging the tables in groups, so the children could work together.

She knew Christopher liked to sharpen pencils, so she left that job for him. He would also enjoy putting the supplies into each desk, so that was something else she didn't have to do.

Tina stopped and looked out through the shiny windows at the schoolyard, imagining how it would look in just a couple of weeks when it would be full of running, shouting children. A shiver of apprehension ran down her spine. Would she be able to meet their educational needs? As well as their emotional ones. She was aware that some of her pupils came from homes where alcohol was used, and she wished the reserve would opt to become dry. That, however, was beyond her mandate. There would have to be other ways she could influence the children's lives.

The composting toilets were one way for they would eliminate the smelly outhouses. The lumber for the new building was already in piles in the yard and the toilets should be arriving any day. Maybe even in time for the beginning of classes. She hoped the children would be interested in creating small vegetable and flower gardens and maybe she could even involve some of the parents to till the soil and help with the weeding.

With a start Tina realized that she was thinking about something that couldn't be accomplished this fall. A garden was a springtime project and an ongoing summer activity. And if she left at Christmas she wouldn't be here to make this happen.

But, of course, nothing was carved in stone. She might stay longer—

"Mommy, Mommy!"

The yell awoke her from her musings. Hazard's truck had pulled into the yard and both fishermen jumped out.

"Look, Mommy!" Christopher ran to her, brandishing a basket with three large fish. He eagerly filled her in on all the relevant details. "They're lake trout!" he shouted, loud enough for anyone within a hundred metres to hear. "I caught them all by myself." One by one he pulled the fish out of the basket and displayed them proudly, holding them by the gills with his bare hands.

This was something Tina never thought she would see him doing, not in her wildest imagination. She clapped her hands in amazement. "You caught them all by yourself?"

Christopher shrugged. "Well, Hazard helped me with the first one and then I knew how to do it," he explained.

"Wow!" Tina threw Hazard a questioning look.

"That's absolutely correct," he confirmed. "He's a quick learner." He tousled Christopher's hair, and Tina saw how fondly he looked at the boy. Hazard obviously really liked her son. The man was a bachelor and she'd assumed he only tolerated Christopher because the reserve needed a teacher, but there seemed to be something of a big buddy-little buddy bond developing between them.

"I'll go into the bush and clean them, now that your mom has had a chance to admire them," Hazard said and took the basket from Christopher. But before he left, the door of the teachers' portable opened and Steve ambled out.

Tina turned her back on him, but Hazard raised a hand in greeting. "How're you doing, Mr. Principal? All ready for the arrival of the hordes?"

"Yep, pretty well ready," Steve replied, sauntering over to join them, still smoking a cigarette.

Sure he was ready. He'd done nothing to his room to show he was anywhere close to being ready to receive his students. Tina's lip curled in disgust. She was aware that Hazard looked at her curiously, but didn't say anything. If Hazard ever asked her about it, she would just say she and Steve hadn't exactly "clicked".

"Hazard wanted to clean them on the shore but then they would've shrunk too small, with the heads chopped off and all. I wanted you to see how big they are," Christopher explained as Hazard walked away with his catch.

"Good thinking, honey," Tina said. "They sure are whoppers."

It didn't take long before Hazard returned with the cleaned fish. "How are you at frying fish, Tina?"

She rolled her eyes. "Hopeless, I'm afraid."

"In that case I'll ask Anna to cook them for us. She can come and do it at my house," Hazard said.

Tina was surprised at this. "But will Anna agree? Maybe she's busy and won't like this job being thrown at her."

"She'll be happy to cook them," Hazard assured

her. "She's been talking about inviting you two over for dinner at her house one day. This is a great chance for her to show off her cooking skills and not have to worry about being the hostess."

"As if she needs to show off her skills," Tina said with a laugh. "We already know she's a superb cook."

"Am I invited, too?" Steve asked. "You really can't talk about Anna's fried trout in front of me and not ask me to join you for dinner." He said it jokingly, but it was obvious to Tina he knew they couldn't refuse.

"Of course, come along," Hazard said. "There's plenty of fish for everyone. I caught a few, too, you know."

Tina wondered if Hazard had any idea of Steve's prejudiced attitude toward the First Nations people, or of his lecherous behavior. At least with her. But she could well imagine that Steve kept his ugliness hidden from the people of the community and put on a genial face when they were around, like he was doing now. The despicable piece of garbage!

Chapter Seven

It turned out Anna was more than happy to cook them a meal of fried fish. By the time Tina and Christopher walked to Hazard's house that evening, the fish were already sizzling in the frying pan, filling the house with an aroma that any fish-lover would appreciate. But Christopher obviously wasn't one of them, because the minute they stepped in he crinkled his nose.

"What's that awful smell?" he asked Tina.

"That's your fish cooking," Tina told him with a laugh. "Wait till you taste it."

"I'm not gonna eat it," he declared vehemently. "Not if it smells that yucky."

But when the fish was on a platter, served with boiled potatoes, buttered carrots and peas, he agreed to take a wee, tiny bite—and immediately fell in love.

The meal was as delicious as any Tina had enjoyed in a fancy Toronto restaurant, but it was marred by the presence of Steve. She didn't want to spoil the party, so she tried her best to appear cordial and not make her dislike of him obvious to anyone. Steve, for his part, was a most winsome charmer, cracking jokes with Hazard and keeping Anna in stitches with his humorous anecdotes of his life in Toronto. Tina smiled as often as she could, but found it difficult, especially when she caught him ogling Anna's ample bosom that jiggled whenever she laughed heartily.

James and Chogan had also been invited for dinner to keep Christopher company, and after they had eaten the three boys ran out to feed bits of fish to Wolf in his cage. Through the screened window Tina heard the boys giggle as the wolf-dog rewarded them by licking their greasy hands.

"Mr. Miller is one funny man," Anna confided to Tina when the two of them were in the kitchen washing up.

Tina felt like responding that funny Mr. Miller almost made her vomit, but refrained from expressing her opinion. She could see Anna was relishing the attentions of the respected school principal, and Tina hoped Steve wouldn't try anything that would betray Anna's trust in him.

Later that evening Hazard drove Tina and the three boys home, although Tina waggishly reminded him that everything on the reserve was within walking distance. She was caught off-guard by his candid response.

"I just wanted to spend some time with you," he said and turned to grin at her in the dimness of the truck. Tina's heart gave an extra skip and she swallowed. The man came up with the most unexpected things.

"But I'm here," Christopher announced from the back seat. "And so are James and Chogan."

"I meant you all, without those other people around," Hazard quickly amended, while Tina tried not to laugh. "Just the five of us."

Tina hurried to change the subject. "The fish was absolutely delicious. Out of this world."

"Yes, it was," Christopher agreed. "We'll go fishing again, right Hazard?"

"We sure will, buddy."

"And James and Chogan can come, too."

"Of course."

It was very pleasant sitting next to Hazard again in the truck. The previous week had passed with no contact, with him being off on a hunting trip, and Tina had to admit she'd missed him. This surprised her, considering how busy she'd been working on her classroom and lesson plans. She'd even scrubbed the tubular metal chair legs with steel wool, so they now shone brightly and showed every scratch and dent that had previously been hidden by dirt.

Each night, when Tina had time to think, Hazard pushed himself into her thoughts. She'd stopped wondering why, having decided it was because it was good to talk with another adult. Especially a hazardously handsome one, which made thinking about him even more pleasant.

On his return from the hunt Hazard had dropped by to see the classroom. The worn patches on the old linoleum now showed up clearly on the clean floor, and it was possible to see that its original colour had actually been a mottled sort of green.

"Don't you think the floor looked better before?" Hazard had joked. "When it was a uniform dirty gray."

"Right," Tina had replied with a laugh. "It does look a lot more splotchy now, doesn't it?" She had batted her eyelashes and looked demurely at him in a blatantly seductive manner. "You're sure you won't consider getting new linoleum this fall? Hmm?"

But he'd only laughed at her and shook his head.

Hazard thought about all that now as Tina sat beside him in the truck. Christopher and the brothers were chatting and joking loudly in the back.

"So you'd like to have a new linoleum for the portables?" he began.

Tina looked at him, her brown eyes bright with surprise. "Yes, of course I would."

"I was thinking that maybe we could free up some money and get some. Linoleum isn't that expensive."

Tina clapped her hands. "Oh, that would be wonderful. You're right, linoleum isn't too expensive. You think you might do that?"

"We'll see," he mused, not wanting to commit himself before looking into it more closely. Tina, he knew, would be ready to order the stuff first thing in the morning, if he even breathed half a syllable that sounded like it was a done deal.

"Just think, a clean floor!" she breathed, throwing back her head in pretend ecstasy. "So nice for the kids, walking on their sock feet."

Hazard laughed. "I think their we'll leave it for now, till I have a chance to consult the elders."

He stopped the truck in front of Tina's home and cut the motor. The boys jumped out and James and Chogan ran up the road to their home, while Christopher went to give Mutt some bits of fish he'd brought with him in a plastic bag.

Hazard undid his seatbelt. Was that enough of a hint to show her he wanted to be invited in?

Obviously it was.

"Are you too tired after a long day of fishing, or do you want to come in for a glass of wine or some coffee?" she asked.

"Coffee would be good," Hazard said and hopped out, happy his trick had worked.

Soon they sat at the kitchen table, face to face, with steaming coffee mugs in front of them. With a belly full of fish, and having got up so early, Christopher had gone to bed without a murmur.

Hazard leaned both elbows on the table. He wanted to get to the bottom of something that had puzzled him all day. "There seems to be something going on between you and Steve," he began.

"I'm sorry," Tina said and her face coloured. "I didn't realize it showed."

That was a sure sign that something was brewing. Of course it could be she was just pretending to dislike him in order to not show she actually was interested in him, but he didn't think she was into such games.

"I tried to be friendly tonight," Tina said. "But I guess I didn't do a very good job of it."

"On the contrary, you were very friendly," Hazard assured her. "But I had a feeling you were too friendly, and something wasn't quite right."

She sat, picking at the chair cushion, which always made him want to smile. But not this time.

"Yes," she finally admitted. "He didn't do anything too terrible, but I just wanted to make sure he understood that I don't appreciate such things."

Hazard felt anger well up inside him. He clenched his jaws but didn't ask. It was obvious she was referring to something sexual.

"I don't want to get him in trouble," she continued. "It was only some . . . some stupid adolescent groping. He probably thought it would be okay between two adults, but I made sure he knew it was not."

The thought of Steve groping Tina made his blood boil. "I'll report him to the police and make sure he gets charged."

"Oh, no, please don't do that. I told him never to touch me again and I'm sure he never will. He's not an idiot. I don't want to ruin his teaching career over this. Let's just drop it. Okay?"

Hazard didn't like the idea, but decided to go along with her request. After all, he'd never heard anything negative about the fellow in the two years Steve had been teaching at the rez. Maybe the sight of a pretty blond woman had just made him a little careless. After all—he had to admit—Tina had sent his own thoughts along similar paths. He certainly wouldn't have minded kissing those lips, or holding her in his arms, feeling her curves under his hands. What normal man wouldn't? But he was no fool. He would never invade her space unless she indicated she would welcome it.

Which she would never do. She was such a mother and didn't seem to need a man. Or maybe it was just the men on the rez she didn't want to have any dealings with. Like him.

Oh, boo-hoo, poor Hazard, feeling sorry for himself. He looked at Tina, so beautiful across the table from him, and remembered how he'd held her after the accident. She'd leaned against him, and . . . Hazard winced . . . then he'd called her "darling". Could he have been more of an idiot?

"Well, I guess I should hit the road." He rose and

placed his mug in the sink. Enough of these useless thoughts. She was returning to Toronto and picking up her former life where she left off. Better not start anything that would leave him hurting. Although unfortunately it looked like that was too late. He already knew he would miss her when she went away. A lot.

Hazard walked slowly to his truck, but instead of climbing in he stood, leaning his forehead against the door. Already the thought of her leaving made his stomach hurt. Or maybe it was his chest? Heart? Whatever. But somewhere deep inside him there was something that was already starting to ache.

And she hadn't even left.

Tina sat on the porch in the afternoon sun, writing in her daily plan book. Wanting to work outside she'd dragged the small coffee table out from the living room and now sat on a lawn chair, making plans for activities for the fall term. She smiled to herself, thinking how this set-up was a far cry from her office in her parents' home. It was incredible how one could get accustomed to pretty near anything.

Only a week remained before school would open, so in the past few days she had spent some time every evening going over simple addition and subtraction facts with Christopher, as well as listening to him read. She felt guilty for having neglected this part of his daily life since coming to Greenstone. At home he'd read to her or to one of his grandparents every evening and had practiced his number facts.

But there were only so many hours in a day, and she spent the biggest part of them cleaning and preparing her classroom and making up worksheets that she then photocopied and made into booklets for her students. She had found no phonics or arithmetic workbooks for any grade level and had even approached Steve to ask if there might be some stacked away somewhere. There weren't.

Christopher spent most of every day playing with Mutt and his two friends, running and climbing outdoors, which more than made up for any math drills. The boys had built a tree house at the far end of the yard and often dug in bogs and ditches for frogs and other slimy creatures. It was a wonder to behold, seeing him holding a snail or an earthworm in his muddy hands. His white skin had tanned nicely and there were fewer red bumps on his arms because most of the biting insects seemed to have disappeared along with the last days of August. What a blessing that was, although they had been replaced with hoards of late summer houseflies. It seemed there was always something buzzing around.

Whenever they Skyped with his grandparents, Christopher told them about his activities with great excitement. Even now Tina grinned when she thought how horrified her mother had looked when, one by one, he proudly took out little slimy creatures from the jar where he had stored them in readiness for "show and tell". Her father always laughed loudly at the offerings, but Tina could tell it was his "jolly fellow" laugh, which he used when he wasn't totally comfortable with a situation. Christopher's dirty fingernails and his hair, which was getting too long to comb off to one side, produced disapproving comments from his Nana.

"How can you let him run around looking like

that?" she said when Christopher had skipped off and was out of earshot. "Those dirty hands can't be healthy, especially after he was wounded. And that disheveled hair looks unkempt."

But at the moment it wasn't Tina's number one priority to visit Yvette, who had told Tina—in her strong French accent, and with considerable pride—that she had apprenticed in Big Thunder.

"Before school begins," she'd promised her mother, and herself, "Christopher and I will pay a visit to Yvette's Salon."

Tina was relieved to see that James and Chogan had turned out to be responsible playmates for Christopher, and allowed him to tag along behind them and learn new things about outdoors. Still, whenever the boys went fishing off the dock, she insisted that Christopher wear a life jacket. Their house was only about a hundred metres from the lake, and if the windows were open, she could hear his excited shouts when one of them caught a fish.

And then there was Hazard. Trustworthy and reliable Hazard. She tried not to feel resentful when Christopher took his word as gospel truth over her opinions, because Hazard was, after all, knowledgeable about everything that had to do with life at the rez. Christopher automatically looked to up him, and—Tina frowned and chewed on the end of her pencil—she had begun to lean on him, too.

That was the problem. It went totally against the goal she'd set for herself. She'd come up here to prove to herself and to her parents that she was able to take care of herself and Christopher without relying on their help. Or anyone else's for that matter. And now it looked like she was in the process of transferring her reliance from her parents to dependable old Hazard.

Damn! She must make sure that from now on she wouldn't run to him every time she needed a job done. Like chopping wood for the woodstove in the living room. Or, as she would have to do this weekend, asking him to drive with her to Big Thunder to pick up her new car.

It was just too convenient to call on Hazard. She slammed down her pencil and snorted with annoyance when the lead broke. From now on she would split her own firewood and Christopher could carry it inside. There was absolutely no reason why they couldn't manage together. Except for that car pick-up. Damn.

"Mommy!" Christopher galloped up the stairs to the porch, followed by Mutt, who wagged its bushy tail and stuck its cold, wet nose against Tina's bare arm.

"Mutt, stop that!" Tina said sternly, but gave its ears a rub.

"Remember when Hazard said he would take me canoeing?" Christopher asked and flopped down on the top stair by Tina's feet, while Mutt sat comfortably with its head on his lap. "He said he'll teach me to paddle."

"Hey, I could teach you to paddle if we had a canoe," Tina said. "I learned to canoe at the summer camp I went to for several years."

She expected Christopher to get excited about her revelation, but instead he brushed this information aside. "Yeah, but Hazard has a canoe, so he can take me."

Well, wasn't that just dandy! Her son thought so little of her skills. She would show him. "We can borrow Hazard's canoe and go out together."

"I wanna go with Hazard," Christopher insisted, his voice turning into a whine. "He's better."

"And how do you know that? I'm pretty good, too, you know." She tried to swallow down the resentment that was welling up inside her.

"He's an Indian and they are good canoers. They even invented canoes," Christopher replied.

Tina didn't want to question his logic. Instead she gathered up her papers and got up. She would show him she was every bit as good at canoeing as Hazard. Maybe even better.

"I'll ask Hazard to loan us his canoe," she said on her way indoors. "Come on, it's time to set the table for dinner."

But first she would once again have to ask for his help to get to Big Thunder. Wasn't there anyone else she could ask to drive her? It wasn't like she didn't always enjoy his company, because she did, but since she had just made the decision to be more self-reliant, she didn't want to run to him with this problem.

She stirred the chili and considered her options, which were almost nil. Definitely not Steve. Maybe Anna's husband? Yes, she could ask Harold. Except what would Hazard think if she didn't ask him? Would he consider her rude? Or would he be relieved not to have to drive that long distance again?

Yes, more than likely he would be happy not to have to go. Tina filled two bowls with thick, steaming chili and placed them on the table, where Christopher had already poured milk into glasses and put out their side plates, spoons and butter knives. She would tell Hazard she didn't want to bother him with another drive to Big Thunder and would instead pay Harold to make the trip. Surely Hazard would be delighted to be let off the hook.

But when Tina dropped by his office and told Hazard of her idea, he didn't look as pleased as she'd expected. She sat with one hip on his desk while he leaned back in his chair.

"I don't know if Harold's truck is in good enough condition to make the trip all the way to Big Thunder and back," he mused.

She had never even considered such a possibility. "You think so? But it's only four hundred kilometres, and back again."

"That's eight hundred kilometres of straight driving. I'm not sure it's such a good idea, not in that vehicle."

Of course he could've loaned his truck to Harold, but Tina didn't think it was her place to suggest it.

"But maybe his son could drive," Hazard continued. "George is young and a good driver. I wouldn't hesitate loaning my truck to him."

"And you couldn't loan it to Harold because . . .?"

Hazard shrugged. "He's got some bad habits. He might be tempted to visit some bars while in Big Thunder."

"Oh." Another possibility she hadn't considered.

"George is a good kid," Hazard said. "He's about twenty-five, and only drinks at parties."

"Super!" Tina hopped off the desk. "That's settled then. If you tell him about the truck, I'll ask him if he's willing to drive it." But somehow, perversely, she wasn't totally happy with the way this had turned out. Hazard had agreed much too readily to let someone else take her. It sounded like he was only too delighted to be off the hook.

Well, wasn't that exactly what she'd wanted to happen? Tina turned to go. All right, then, she would never ask him to help her out again. With anything.

Hazard came from around the desk and standing behind her, placed his hands on her shoulders.

"I would, of course, have offered to take you myself, but—"

She turned quickly to face him. "Hey, you already did a huge job driving me there once. It wouldn't be fair, asking you to do it again."

"As I said I would've done it, except—"

"Please, Hazard," she put up a hand to stop him. "You don't have to explain your reasons. I understand."

He took her face between his hands and the blood rushed into her head, making the pulse at her temples beat furiously.

"No, you don't understand, Tina," Hazard said, his voice dangerously low. "You aren't letting me explain."

"But I said there's no need to explain." She pulled herself free. "What you do with your time is not my business. Just like what I do with mine is—"

Again he took hold of her shoulders and gave her a gentle shake. "I get it, I get it! But I still want to tell you why I can't come. Much as I would love to drive four hundred kilometres with you sitting there beside me—"

He stopped, looking slightly abashed, and then released her. "Okay, don't look so shocked. It just came out. Sorry."

Tina's heart was in turmoil. His words had opened

the floodgates for her own emotions to come pouring out, and she didn't know where to look, what to say to him. Because that was how she also felt. It would have been wonderful to sit beside him all the way to Big Thunder, even with Christopher chattering in the back. She hadn't wanted to admit this to herself, but now she knew this was exactly what she had secretly been hoping for.

"Tina?" Gently he raised her chin and made her look deep into the shining black pools of his eyes.

"Okay," she whispered. "So, tell me."

Hazard still held her chin to keep her looking up at him, and his voice was deep and smooth as he spoke. "One of the kids on the reserve is getting out of prison. I promised his mother I would fly to Winnipeg to bring him home. She doesn't trust anyone else to get him because he might not want to come back. Unfortunately that's happening the same day you're scheduled to get your car. Otherwise I would have driven with you."

"I understand. And I'm sorry." Her eyes had lowered to gaze at his mouth as he spoke and she was only vaguely aware of what he had told her. His lips were too close. And then they were no longer close, because she felt them on hers, barely touching. It was incredible how soft that firm mouth could feel.

The kiss was so light it almost wasn't there, and she found herself wanting more. She opened her lips ever so slightly, and immediately he answered her signal.

He took her face between his hands. "Tina," he groaned.

His kiss deepened and as she opened her mouth to

him, his tongue entered. The force of the kiss shook her to her very core. And then his arms were around her, holding her tightly against him. This was what she'd been dreaming of when she lay in bed—being in Hazard's arms. But she never expected it would happen. Because it was not supposed to happen.

"I'm not staying, you know," she whispered against his mouth.

He raised his head and looked into her eyes. "I know," he murmured.

"I don't want you to get hurt."

He shook his head. "I'll look after myself." And then the dark pools that were his eyes closed, and he kissed her again, with a passion that filled every fibre of her being. It left her weak, but wanting more. Much more.

She didn't want this to end, but it was daylight and they were in his office, and—

"Oh, my goodness!" Tina exploded out of his arms. "I have to pick up Christopher. He's at Anna's, and I'm late."

"What's he doing at Anna's?"

The hand he ran through his hair wasn't totally steady.

"It's her day off and she's teaching him how to make bread."

Hazard's deep laughter burst out. "Really?"

"Yes. He loves her bread and wanted to know how to make it, so he could make it at home." Had they really just kissed passionately, and now were discussing her son's bread-making?

They walked out of the building together and stood on the front steps.

"Why doesn't he just go over to her house and buy

some?" Hazard asked.

Tina laughed. "He wants to make sure he has it fresh whenever he wants it. I'm sure this lesson will show him that it's not as simple as he imagined it to be, but I figured it's good for him to see how much work there is to bread-making."

"Good idea. Now he won't take every slice for granted," Hazard agreed. "But before I go to Winnipeg, I'll speak with George and make sure he's okay driving you to Big Thunder. That okay with you?"

"Of course. If you think—" There she was, doing it again, asking for his opinion and having him call the shots. "Sure. That's fine," she snapped.

A puzzled look flashed across his face. "I'll call you," he said and stood on the steps while she started off at a brisk pace toward Anna's house.

Just then she remembered something and turned around. "Oh, by the way, I'd like to borrow your canoe one of these days when you're not using it."

A few moments later Tina stepped inside Anna's modest three-bedroom bungalow, where she lived with her husband, Harold, and their son, George. The house was similar to most of the others on the reserve, except now the delicious aroma of freshly-baked bread filled the home. In the middle of the kitchen stood Christopher, a huge yellow apron wrapped around his middle, beaming proudly.

"Mommy, look at the bread I made!" He ran to the counter and grabbed one of the loaves.

"Careful, it's hot," Anna said, but laughed at his enthusiasm. "He's a fine baker," she said to Tina. "He learns very quickly."

"Yes, probably it has something to do with the fact

that he loves to eat your bread," Tina said. "He doesn't learn his number facts nearly as quickly." Gingerly she took the loaf that Christopher held out to her and sniffed the crust. "Ahh! There can't be anything as delicious as the smell of freshly baked bread."

Anna's easy laughter rang out again. She laughed a lot, Tina had noted, which made it pleasant to be in her company.

"It smells good, doesn't it? Now Christopher can make it at home whenever he wants," Anna said.

Tina put a hand on her son's shoulder. "Really? So you actually know how to make bread now?"

Christopher nodded eagerly. "Anna showed me how to use the bread-making machine. And she's going to let me borrow it any time I want."

Tina nodded. "Oh, okay. That explains it. Maybe when we're in Big Thunder we'll buy one for you, so Anna can keep hers safe from harm."

Chapter Eight

George was a shy, handsome youth, and more than surpassed the stereotypical idea Tina had once had of the "silent Indian". On the way to Big Thunder not ten words came out of his mouth directed at her. She had tried to keep up a conversation, but it soon had become obvious that it was totally one-sided. So instead she spent most of her time looking at the scenery. She was surprised how fond she was growing of this rugged, silent land. There was something incredibly primitive in the untouched rivers and lakes and the spindly spruce that somehow defied the hostile conditions in which they grew.

Why did this make her think of Hazard? Although maybe thinking about him had nothing to do with the scenery and everything to do with what had transpired between them only two short days ago. Thinking about the kiss still made the blood rush through her.

But Christopher, hurtling an unending stream of questions at George, kept her from falling too deeply into reverie. And George had to keep replying to the little inquisitioner. Tina had chosen not to take James and Chogan along, because she didn't want to put the responsibility on George to deal with them on the way back. And she sure wasn't about to drive home in her new car with three noisy boys in the back seat. One Christopher was more than enough.

"George, what do you do at the reserve?" she asked.

The fellow coughed and blushed. "Fish and hunt," he replied.

"Do you ever think about getting a trade?"

"Yeah," was his laconic reply.

"What trade are you thinking of?"

"Dunno."

This was like trying to milk a bull. "Do you like working with electricity?" she tried.

"Nah."

"With plumbing?"

"Nah."

"With wood?" Tina tried again, beginning to grow desperate.

"Yeah."

Bingo! She'd struck gold. "Carpentry?"

George shook his head. "Carving."

"Carving? Carving what?" She was afraid his answer might require too many words.

"Things."

Boy, the fellow sure had a gift for giving one sweeping answer to a question. She tried again. "What kinds of things?"

George blushed deeply. "Like moose, 'n' fish, 'n' birds. Things like that."

This was getting interesting. "You carve these figures out of wood?"

"Yeah."

Christopher was curious, too, and poked his head

up between them from the back seat as far as his seat-belt would allow. "What do you do with them?"

"Just keep 'em."

"To me it sounds like you're an artist," Tina decided. "Right?"

George looked down at his hands on the steering wheel. "Kinda."

It was obvious the young man was embarrassed by having made this revelation. But what Tina had discovered excited her.

"When we get back home, do you think you could show me your carvings? I really would like to see them. But only if you're okay with that."

A long silence followed.

Tina didn't want to make him feel any more embarrassed and decided not to prod him for an answer. But Big Thunder was getting closer and closer and it was beginning to look like George wouldn't reply before they got there. Tina took that to mean he was not eager to show his work to her.

But at long last came the reply. "Yeah."

He had obviously thought it through very carefully. Tina smiled as she looked out the window. "Okay. You tell me when."

"Are you sure you don't want me to come canoeing with you?" Hazard asked. Of course he had given his permission for her to use his canoe, but it didn't sound to Tina like he trusted her skills. They stood on the shore of Stony Lake and the canoe was already in the water. Christopher sat in it, wearing a life jacket.

Tina clipped on her vest. "Yes, I particularly want to go canoeing without you," she replied.

"We could both paddle," he persisted. "It's quite windy out there."

"It's fine out there. I've been out in much windier conditions."

"But—" Hazard threw up his arms in resignation. "Okay, as you wish."

Tina got into the stern of the canoe and pushed it off the shore. "It has to do with independence. You wouldn't understand."

"I'd call it stubbornness myself," Hazard called back.

"Mommy, are you sure you know how to handle this?" Christopher held onto the gunwales with white knuckles.

Well, of all the—! How dare he doubt her skills. "I went to camp every summer. I've told you that, Christopher."

"Yeah, but I forget. And I don't know what you did there."

"I told you I canoed."

"Yeah, but I forget."

Of course she understood that all those months of carefree camp life were only in her own memory, and telling anecdotes about it hadn't brought it to life for her son.

As Tina paddled, the canoe slid effortlessly through the water. She hadn't done any canoeing since Christopher had arrived on the scene, probably because she hadn't wanted to take the toddler out in a canoe by herself. No, that was no excuse. Her parents had always filled in whenever she'd wanted to do something on her own. For several years water sports simply had no longer held a place of priority in her life.

Not like in her teens when she and her friends had fooled around in every kind of water craft at the cottage.

And now all that fun was ahead for him to experience for himself!

"I think you should go to camp next summer when we're back home," Tina said. "You can learn to canoe and build campfires, and all sorts of fun stuff." She expected an automatic "Yea!", but instead he frowned.

"I don't need to go to camp," he said. "I know how to make a fire. James and Chogan showed me. And Hazard can teach me to canoe."

"I told you I can teach you to canoe," Tina snapped and immediately was sorry.

The boy's lower lip began to wobble. "But I want Hazard to teach me."

Stubborn kid! "Listen, here's a paddle for you." With her toe she pushed a smaller paddle, lying on the bottom of the canoe, toward him. "Take that and I'll show you how to—"

"No! I don't wanna!" The cry rang out over the lake and Tina realized, to her dismay, that Hazard—and anyone else who might be on the shore—could hear it.

"Hush, Christopher," she whispered. "Sound carries over the water really well. Everybody can hear you crying."

"I'm not crying," Christopher muttered sulkily. "I just don't wanna paddle." His brows were puckered in a very angry frown.

"But you said you wanted to learn."

"I said I want Hazard to teach me."

With a deft move Tina spun the canoe around. Totally unreasonable fury boiled inside her. Was it directed at Christopher for doubting her, or at Hazard for having upstaged her? Or maybe it was directed at herself for behaving childishly? And for having fallen under the spell of the handsome chief?

Because since their kisses, she hadn't had one good night's sleep. How could she sleep, with images of the man floating through her brain, and with her body aching for closer contact with him. His deep kisses had promised something wonderfully exciting.

Tina beached the canoe onto the sandy shore and then jumped out, leaving Christopher to struggle on his own in the tippy canoe. It was about time the boy learned some independence.

Hazard was still standing where they'd left him only a few minutes ago. "Well, that was a short canoe trip," he said and Tina saw he was trying not to smile. Of course he'd heard every word between them.

"Mommy, help me!" Christopher stood in the teetering canoe, and reached out his hand for her. "I'm going to fall in the water."

Tina's hesitated for only a moment, but in that time Hazard stepped into the water and lifted the boy out.

"I think he should learn to do things for himself,' she muttered and promptly began to undo the buckles on his life jacket.

Christopher stepped back, his face a picture of indignation. "I can do that myself!" he cried.

And he did, while Tina stood there, feeling like an idiot. Couldn't she say anything that made sense? First telling the child to be independent and then starting to unbuckle his lifejacket? What kind of a school teacher did Hazard think she was? A wishy-washy nutcake?

She undid her vest and tossed it in the canoe.

"Okay, time to go home for lunch," she said brightly, pretending everything was all right. "We were going to have a picnic on that little island." She pointed to a rock that could hardly be called more than a shoal. "But since Christopher didn't want to—"

"I didn't say I didn't want to have a picnic. I just didn't want to paddle," Christopher corrected her, again making her feel foolish.

"Whatever." Reaching into the canoe, Tina picked up the picnic basket and marched off. Since Hazard was so keen to help the boy, he could carry him all the way home on his back, if he wished.

Hazard looked after her and then turned around to show Christopher how to tip the canoe over for storage. The boy was so eager to learn it almost hurt.

"Let's go and see if your mom will give us something from that picnic basket," he suggested and together they took off after Tina. As they walked, Hazard felt Christopher's hand slip into his, and his heart squeezed in a strange, new way.

Tina was obviously angry about something, and although Hazard suspected this anger was directed at him, he had no idea what he'd done to deserve it.

Women! He wished the hell she would just spit it out and clarify any issues she had. That would have been easier than trying to second-guess what the problem was. Was she angry with him because of the kiss? He had to admit he was far from comfortable with it, himself. He'd dreamt about kissing her before, but now, having tasted her lips and feeling her slender body against him, his dreams had gone way beyond kissing. He'd undressed her and made wild love to her. And awakened in a heavy sweat.

Sure, he'd told her not to worry about him because he could take care of himself, but he knew that wouldn't be easy. The thought of her leaving caused a deep ache inside him, and the idea of having to live with that hurt for the rest of his life didn't sit well with him at all. Who liked to live in pain?

Damn these complications! He didn't need them in his life, which was already complicated enough with this new job as the chief. It was something that had almost been thrust upon him, and he'd been unable to say no when the elders had approached him on his return from Kingston. He'd come home to stay a while, visit with friends and family and relax after five arduous years of study. His plan had been to return south with his business degree and apply for jobs in the environmental field. But now he was trapped, and was responsible for making all kinds of vital decisions regarding the future of the people of Greenstone.

Right now things weren't going that well. After the previous chief had been caught using the federal funds to line his own pockets, the people were pretty annoyed, and looked to him to make things better. Yeah, like how? He knew he definitely needed to find something meaningful for the young fellows to do. They'd finished school and now hung around Harold's Diner all day. But what could they do, besides going fishing pretty near every day and hunting now and then?

Add to this mix a headstrong woman who had arrived with outrageous ideas. Like composting toilets, for God's sake.

Although actually they weren't such a bad idea. In

fact, building the new outhouse provided some meaningful activity for some of the guys, as well as for Joe Wind Song, who supervised them.

Good fellow, that Joe. He could do just about any job from carpentry to masonry to electricity. Even plumbing in a pinch. He could teach the young fellows a thing or two. Maybe he could even be persuaded to give a few lessons to them and get paid for his trouble. Something to look into, for sure.

By the time Hazard and Christopher arrived at the house, Tina had taken the food out of the picnic basket and set out plates for the three of them. She didn't look angry any more, unless she was just hiding it under a good-natured facade. Which he didn't like any better. Spit it out, he wanted to say to her. Let's talk.

But not now, with Christopher around. And he was always around. Not much chance for his crazy dreams to come true.

"Did you know that George carves animal figures out of wood?" Tina asked as they dug into the salmon salad sandwiches. "Have you seen them?"

"I know he's always been carving," Hazard said. "Ever since I've known him. But I haven't exactly inspected his work." What was this sudden shift leading to?

"Well, you should. They're very good," she said and moved a milk glass away from Christopher's elbow.

"They're really, really good!" Christopher echoed, his mouth full.

"Christopher, keep your mouth closed when you chew," Tina reprimanded him.

"But then I can't ta-a-lk." Deliberately he opened his mouth to show the food inside, and Hazard had to hold back a chuckle. Tina, he saw, was not amused.

She frowned. "Yes, you can. If you don't take such huge bites."

Of course Hazard had noticed that manners and cleanliness were Tina's big concerns. Too big, in his unexpressed opinion.

"Okay, I'll look at them next time I visit Anna," he said, to get back to the topic they'd been discussing. He was curious to know where Tina was going with this carving thing, but wasn't sure if he really wanted to find out. Her plans had a way of costing money, like composting toilets and new linoleum for the classroom floors. What next?

"Good. I'm going to suggest to him that he put some of them up for sale at a tourist store in Big Thunder. On commission."

The fellow was that good? Hazard really hadn't noticed. "You think anyone would buy them?"

"Yes, I do." She sat, leaning her chin on her hand, while Hazard waited for something else to come. He knew that look on her face which told him she was hatching a plan. It seemed the closer to her he got, the better he was at reading her thoughts. But was getting closer a good idea?

This time, however, she caught him from the left field.

"In fact," she began, "I've been thinking that there are a lot of things on this reserve that are marketable and could earn some money for the people."

"Yeah?" Off-hand he couldn't think of one. "Such as?"

"Well, Anna's baking comes to mind first and foremost," Tina told him. "And I know that Harold, even though you say he drinks, can sew fabulous moccasins. I asked him to make me a pair, now that fall is here."

"Okay. That's true." He knew Harold's work wasn't bad. In fact, he owned a buckskin jacket Harold had made from the hide of a deer Hazard had shot a few years back while home on a break from university.

"There's a First Nations Reserve not hundred and fifty kilometres from Toronto where they have their own market place along the highway."

Okay, so that's where she was going.

"They sell all kinds of things," she went on."I've been there a few times to pick up some lovely, unique gifts."

"We don't happen to have a major highway nearby," Hazard reminded her. "And I've never seen a traffic jam on the road to Spruce Falls."

Naturally Tina wouldn't give up that easily. "True, but in Spruce Falls we could rent one of the empty storefronts on Main Street for peanuts," she persisted.

Hazard had to laugh. "Well, there's plenty of empty storefronts in Spruce Falls, all right. But that's because there's no customers in town."

Tina tapped her fork on the table to emphasize her words. "Yes, but we'd only rent it for the summer and fall when the fishermen and hunters come and pass by there."

Hazard could see the fires of enthusiasm sparkle in her eyes and knew she wouldn't give up till her plan was a reality. Like the composting toilets that were already on their way.

"And to campers," she concluded.

"What campers?"

"The campers that will come to Greenstone because there's beautiful Stony Lake right here where they can canoe and fish. All they need are a few cleared camp-sites where they can pitch their tents. And a few out-houses. Or preferably composting toilets." She smiled, her brown eyes teasing him.

Hazard's head swam. How could talking about toi-lets be so sexy, for God's sake? And she made every-thing sound so easy and simple. But thinking about it in broad daylight . . .? If it was such a great idea, why hadn't they already done it? Could be because the pre-vious chief wasn't interested in initiating anything. It was up to him now. "So what, exactly, are you suggest-ing?"

She looked at him, head tilted to one side, still smiling. Her next words mirrored his thoughts. "You're the chief. You can make things happen." She got up to clear the table. "Christopher, go wash up. You have mustard on your chin."

"I like it there," came the cheeky reply.

Tina turned to look at her son and for a moment Hazard thought she might bark at him. But then she turned and went to put the dishes in the sink."Yes, I agree, you should leave it there," she said. "Adds colour to your face." Then she continued, now speak-ing to Hazard over her shoulder, "And by the way, there are berries and mushrooms in the forest."

"Of course there are. I know that."

"Did you know Tracey makes lovely blueberry jam? She could teach interested ladies how to make it. We could organize classes."

Hazard laughed. "I think you're an impossible dreamer." But wasn't that along the same lines he'd just been thinking with regards to Joe Wind Song? Classes to teach new skills to the young fellows.

She turned to face him, leaning her back against the sink. "Dream big, or go home."

Go home. Confusion flashed in her eyes as she said that. Was it the realization that she wouldn't be around to see it all happen?

These days his big, impossible dreams were always about her. He rose from the table and went to stand in front of her. Ignoring the fact that Christopher was in the house, he placed his hands on her shoulders. "You're right," he murmured. "I should be dreaming big about the future of my people. The trouble is, I just keep dreaming about you."

Tina glanced toward the hallway, to make sure Christopher was in the bathroom. "Hazard, I'll be leaving. I told you I didn't want you to get—"

"I know. Unfortunately my heart doesn't listen too well. It's a bit like Christopher."

Tina shook her head. "Please don't say things like that."

"I won't say a word," he murmured. "I just want to kiss you."

He took her face between his hands and did just that. And she responded, like she always did in his dreams, opening her mouth to him.

His arms went around her and he held her in a tight embrace while his kiss deepened. He wanted so much to make the rest of his dreams come true, and the way her arms slipped up around his neck, pulling him closer, he knew she had those same dreams.

School started. Into her sparkling portable, Tina

welcomed eighteen pupils ranging from kindergarten to grade three. New light green linoleum shone on the floor and the walls were freshly painted a warm lemon-yellow to cover the sickly green. That was another concession she's wrung out of Hazard, and Joe Wind Song had shown a few young men how to use paint rollers. She had hung curtains with small flowered prints on the windows. The desks were clean, although gouged and scarred by years of wear, and inside each was a pencil, an eraser and a new box of crayons.

Tina greeted each child with a smile and spent the first morning reading a story to them from a picture book and teaching them a new song. They chatted about their summer activities, and then she set them to draw a picture of themselves to put up on the wall with their names.

At lunch time the children walked home while Christopher and Tina sat outside on the portable steps eating their sandwiches. The day was sunny and incredibly warm for the first week of September and autumn flies buzzed around them. Tina decided to change her plans and have a gym class outside instead of doing math and printing. Might was well take advantage of the lovely weather that was bound to turn cool any day.

"So, how many kids had to be sent home?"

Steve appeared around the corner and Tina felt like a dark cloud had just eclipsed the sun.

"No one had to be sent home," Christopher replied. "We had fun. And I'm in grade one now," he announced proudly.

"Well, bully for you," Steve responded.

Tina hoped Christopher didn't understand the

man's sarcastic tone. She wanted to tell Steve to disappear, but couldn't show such bad manners in front of her son.

"How was your morning?" she instead asked, forcing her voice to sound civil.

"Just dandy," Steve said. "Dandy. A couple of lugs showed up an hour late. I told them where to get off."

"What are lugs?" Christopher asked.

Tina hurried to answer before Steve had a chance to say anything rude. "They're a type of nut," she said. "You put them at the end of a bolt. And then you screw the bolt on."

Steve's laugh was ugly. "You're right on, there! They're nuts, all right. And screwing's what they do best, because they're not much good at anything else."

Tina got up from the step and gathered up their sandwiches into the lunch box. "We're going for a walk," she told Christopher.

"I haven't finished eating," the boy complained.

"You can finish later," she snapped. "We need the exercise."

Steve laughed again and the sound grated in her ears. "You want me to accompany you?"

"No, thank you," Tina said sharply. She could barely control her temper.

They walked off with Steve's harsh laughter sweeping the schoolyard.

Pity the kids in his class.

Chapter Nine

A couple of weeks later, as Tina was getting ready to pack up for the day, there was a timid knock on the portable door. It was so quiet that at first Tina thought she had only imagined the sound. Then it came again.

She put down her pen. "Come in," she said. Who could this be? School was out an hour ago. Christopher had gone home with James and Chogan and would spend some time playing in their yard under Florence's supervision, although Tina still wasn't totally comfortable letting him go off without her.

The door opened and a dark head peeked in. "Mrs. Lawrence?"

It was Charlotte from Steve's class. Tina had seen her during recess and had noted that she was always alone and didn't join her classmates in the skipping games. She'd assumed the girl felt she was too big for such games, being tall and well developed. A pretty girl, she was perhaps fourteen years old and in grade eight.

Tina got up to welcome her. "Come in, Charlotte."

The girl's red and puffy face told her this was not going to be a happy session. Tina led her to sit in one of the little chairs and then sat opposite her, but not too close, so the child would have some space.

"What's the problem, Charlotte?" she asked gently, but for a few moments there was only the sound of ragged breathing as Charlotte visibly fought for control of her emotions.

Finally she sighed deeply and looked down at her hands, clasped tightly on her lap. "I'm in trouble."

"In trouble?" What could the girl have done to get her in such trouble that she'd be crying about it?

"Yes."

"Can you tell me about it? Maybe I can help."

"Can you?" Charlotte looked up at Tina with eyes that were shining with tears and hope.

"I hope so, but first you have to let me know what the trouble is."

Charlotte sighed again and sat for a while, staring down at her hands. "It's Mr. Miller," she said.

"Mr. Miller?" Tina's skin began to crawl with a horrible premonition. She prayed she was wrong.

"Did he do something to you?" The words had to be forced out through a choking lump in her throat.

"Yeah." Charlotte looked up at Tina again and this time there was fear in her eyes. "He told me not to say anything. Please don't let him know I told you," she cried. "He'll be so angry, he'll hit me again."

"He hit you?" Tina hoped against hope that this was all the man had done.

"Yes. Every time afterwards he smacked me really hard and said if I tell anybody I'll be in trouble. But now I have to tell, because I am in trouble and—" Charlotte burst out crying. "I don't know who else I can tell!"

Every time afterwards. Her "trouble" could only mean one thing. "Charlotte, are you pregnant?" Tina asked gently.

The girl sobbed. "Yeah."

"Mr. Miller did this to you?"

"Yeah." Charlotte looked up. "I didn't want to because I knew it was a bad thing to do," she said earnestly. "But he hit me and he . . . he kept doing it." She burst out crying. "I should have stayed home and not come to school, but he said I have to come or I'd be in bigger trouble. So I came and he kept me after school and I couldn't say anything." She stifled a sob. "I'm so ashamed."

"You have no reason to be ashamed, Charlotte, because you didn't do anything wrong. It wasn't your fault, it's his. You're just a child and he's a grown man. A big bully." She reached over and stroked the girl's shoulder to comfort and calm her, while her own insides roiled with pure fury. That bastard! That lowdown rat!

Guilt tore at her. She should have reported him when she saw what a letch he was. She shouldn't have worried about his teaching career when he'd tried to push himself onto her in the storage closet. What a fool she'd been. She could have prevented him from abusing Charlotte during the past two weeks if only she had done something before school started, before he began to assault Charlotte. Dear Lord, why hadn't she done anything?

"When did he first do this to you?" Tina asked. Her heart hammered with anger and she tried to keep her hands from shaking.

"Last spring. Before the summer holidays. And now

he's started it again."

Quickly Tina calculated how far along Charlotte's pregnancy could be. As much as four months. It was time she saw a doctor.

Charlotte's next words dropped on her like a bombshell.

"Mrs. Lawrence, can you take the baby?"

"What?" Tina didn't mean to sound shocked, but the question was shot at her totally from the left field.

To her chagrin it set Charlotte sobbing violently. "I knew you wouldn't help." She started to get up.

"Charlotte, of course I'll help you," Tina said soothingly, and put out a hand to make her sit down again. "You just caught me by surprise, that's all. I expect when you tell your mother about this, she'll help you with the baby."

"I can't tell my mother," Charlotte sobbed. She crouched over like a wounded animal.

"Of course you can. And I'm sure she'll help you with this. Just like my parents helped me with my baby when I became pregnant with Christopher."

She hadn't meant to reveal anything, but then was glad she did, because a spark of interest temporarily replaced the sadness in Charlotte's big, black eyes.

"You got knocked up, too?" the girl asked in amazement.

Despite everything, Tina had to smile. "No, I didn't get knocked up. Not exactly. Not the way it happened to you. I was a grown woman at the time, but the man and I weren't married," Tina explained, wondering if she was telling too much. But she then decided to go on. "Christopher was an unplanned baby and we had no intention of getting married. So my parents stepped up to help me. I lived with them until I came here."

"He didn't love you?"

"We didn't love each other. Not the way two people should love each other if they want to spend the rest of their lives together." Tina had no idea if Charlotte understood about people having sex just for the pleasure of it, and she hoped she wouldn't have to go there. "If you tell your mother exactly what you told me," she went on, "your mother will see it was Mr. Miller who was bad and not you. You can tell her he raped you. She'll understand and help you."

"No. My mother wouldn't be helpful. She drinks too much," Charlotte explained. "It's the baby I'm worried about, because I know our house isn't a good place for it."

Tina could see Charlotte had thought this out very carefully before approaching her, and was telling the facts like they were. It was no use trying to convince her otherwise. Charlotte knew her mother and was facing the truth in a grown-up way.

But what was Tina to do now? Tell Hazard, of course, and he would see that Steve was charged with rape. But then what?

"Charlotte, I'm not going to be staying at Greenstone very long," she said, keeping her voice as gentle as possible.

"So will you take the baby with you?"

Tina blanched. What could she say? "I'll probably leave before the baby is born," she quickly replied. That meant she would leave at Christmas. Even if she might be planning to stay till June, in this situation leaving at Christmas seemed like the best thing to do. "Besides, I don't think you'll want to give up your baby," she stammered, mentally crossing her fingers.

Charlotte stood up, as though the matter were settled. "Yes, I do. My baby will be happy with you. You're a good teacher and a very kind lady. All the kids in your class tell me how nice you are."

Tina also stood up and walked to the window. It was late afternoon and the sun was getting ready to set.

"Thank you. It's kind of you to say so, but—"

"If your mom took care of you and Christopher, maybe she could help take care of my baby, too."

Tina almost burst out laughing. She could imagine her mother's reaction if she showed up with an infant in her arms. A brown-skinned baby with eyes as black as night.

That's what her baby would look like if Hazard were the father. Lord! Where were her thoughts straying? She must concentrate on Charlotte and her predicament. She went to the girl and put an arm around her shoulders. "I know it took a lot of courage to come and tell me about this, Charlotte, especially when you're scared about what Mr. Miller would do to you." She gave the girl a gentle squeeze. "I'm very glad you came. I want you to go home now and not worry. If it's all right with you, I'll have a talk with Mr. Abraham and he'll see that Mr. Miller will never bother you again. Together we'll figure out what is the best thing to do."

Charlotte sniffled. "Thank you, Mrs. Lawrence. I knew you'd help."

Well, she sure owed the girl big time for neglecting to report Steve's sexual advances in late August. Although he had already been molesting Charlotte last spring and Charlotte may already have been pregnant

when the school year ended, still Tina could have prevented him from continuing his abuse this fall. She
could try to convince herself that she didn't know he
would stoop so low as to rape a child, but no amount
of rationalizing would give her an out. She should have
reported him.

After Charlotte left, Tina sat down at her desk,
cradling her head in her arms. How could she have
been so naïve? By playing nice to the louse to save his
career, she'd instead enabled him to continue his horrible activities. It was fortunate that Steve wasn't at
school at this moment or Tina would have rushed over
like an avenging angel and scratched his eyes out.
How many times had she been working in her room,
blissfully preparing lessons or stapling work onto the
bulletin boards, unaware of the awful things that were
going on next door? Guilt stabbed at her heart and
tears filled her eyes. Poor, poor Charlotte.

She continued to sit, as feelings of impotent regret
raged inside her. At last she glanced at the large,
round clock on the wall and shot up. Goodness! She
should have been picking Christopher up long ago.
She didn't want to take advantage of their friendship
and use Florence as a babysitter whenever she had
something "more important" to do.

Another reason to feel guilty.

Abhorrence filled him as Hazard listened to Tina,
and his hands clenched into tight fists. But it wasn't
just directed at Steve. Since returning to Greenstone,
he'd felt an intense dislike for the fellow, but hadn't
looked further into his reasons. He could have ques-
tioned the students about him, but hadn't. It wasn't

easy to get teachers into the school, especially men teachers who were better at handling the difficult junior and intermediate boys. And so he hadn't wanted to do or say anything that might cause Steve to leave.

What kind of a chief was he, not taking care of the most vulnerable people on the reserve?

They sat on the steps of Tina's front porch as the evening sun slowly set into the north-west. A cool breeze had begun to blow from the north so Tina had wrapped a sweater around her shoulders. The porch, however, gave enough protection for them to remain outside.

When she'd called him and asked him to come over, he'd quickly jumped into his truck, looking forward to a relaxing Friday evening in Tina's company. Granted, her voice had sounded too serious, but he'd thought that maybe she just was tired after a week of teaching. School had only been operating for a couple of weeks, and it was possible she hadn't yet built up the stamina necessary for carrying on all day with eighteen busy little ones.

"I blame myself, Hazard," Tina said and rubbed her forehead. "I can't get over the fact that poor Charlotte was abused while I sat nearby in my classroom. I feel so horrible. So guilty."

"It's not your fault, Tina," Hazard said. "I didn't feel right about him when I came back to the reserve in the spring, but I chose to ignore my gut feelings. He was a male teacher and I figured we were lucky to have him so he could handle the older boys. How wrong could I be!"

He got up and circled around in front of the porch in frustration.

"Tina, I feel like such a useless schmuck. What kind of a chief am I if I can't even protect the kids on the reserve?" He sat down again beside her, and through his pain was gratified to feel her hand come up to grip his.

"You've only been a chief for a short while," Tina said. "I know it's difficult not to be hard on yourself, but it's not your fault it happened. Now the thing is to look after Charlotte and make sure Steve gets charged."

"I'll call Spruce Falls tomorrow morning and speak to the RCMP," Hazard told her. "It's better I keep away from Steve because I would pummel him to jelly if I ran across him."

"But what am I going to do about the baby?" Tina asked. "Charlotte wants me to take it and care for it, but I—" She swallowed. "I won't be here."

Hazard tried to find comfort in the slight hesitation. Maybe it meant she was reconsidering her plans? Maybe she was thinking of staying beyond the end of the school year? He didn't dare to hope that she would stay forever, because that was being totally unrealistic. Her home was in Toronto and he was too much of a pragmatist to ever indulge in foolish hopes. Dreams, yes. But hopes? Not a chance.

"If she's four months pregnant, the baby won't be born till around February," Tina said. "But in any case, she has to be seen by a doctor. I can't take time off since there's no teacher to take my place, but maybe you could drive her to Spruce Falls?"

"Sure. If you make the appointment so I won't have to talk to the doctor. I don't think Charlotte would like for me to put my nose into her baby affairs." He looked around. "Where's Christopher tonight?"

"He's gone to spend the evening with James and Chogan," Tina said. "Though I have to admit I'm not too keen on him going into that house."

"Why not?" Hazard suspected he knew the answer.

"It's not very clean, you know. I don't know what he'll be putting in his mouth there." She looked slightly embarrassed. "I know I shouldn't feel that way, but I can't help it. I've spent his whole life trying to keep him healthy. He was such a sickly, tiny baby and I even thought I would lose him at one point."

"But he's a pretty strong little fellow now," Hazard said. "I think you can relax and stop worrying."

"Maybe, but it's hard to just change one's way of thinking all of a sudden, you know." She stood up and leaned on the porch railing, and he joined her. "And here's Charlotte so worried about her unborn child, and wanting it to have a healthy life." She turned to look up at Hazard with concerned eyes. "What can I tell her? I can't take the baby back to Toronto with me."

Hazard wanted to tell her that if she stayed here, the problem would be solved because then she could just keep the baby. Instead he said, "You could tell her that if she agrees to adoption, you'll find a good home for the baby with some very responsible people."

"Yes. I could do that," Tina agreed, brightening up. "Would she be okay with adoption, do you think?"

"Unless, of course, after the baby is born she'll want to keep it."

"But she's much too young to be a mother!" Tina exclaimed. "She'll be only fifteen. She has to go to high school in Spruce Falls, and can't be taking care of a baby. In Toronto there are facilities for pregnant teenagers so they can continue their education, but there are no such things here."

Hazard nodded. "So maybe adoption is the best alternative."

"But she asked me to take it!" Tina cried. "I would be letting her down if I suggested adoption. It would be like me saying I don't want the baby."

"Do you?" He looked down into her eyes, but Tina averted hers.

"Right now, I can't even imagine having to take care of a baby," she admitted quietly. "I know I sound selfish, but . . . I'm sorry, that's how I feel." Her eyes shone with tears. "I just feel so bad about this whole thing. About poor Charlotte having gone through such horror. And here I'm not even prepared to help her by taking the baby."

Her shoulders shook with sobs, and then the flood gates opened and Tina collapsed against his chest, crying desperately. Hazard held her against him, feeling guilty for enjoying the chance to do so.

"I feel awful. I should have reported Steve," Tina sobbed. "And poor Charlotte's had to endure more abuse this fall because of my stupidity."

"Let's go in," he suggested. Someone down the road might see them in this position and get the wrong impression. With his arm around her shoulders, he led her into the kitchen, while Tina continued to sob violently.

Hazard took her in his arms. "You couldn't have imagined—"

"Yes, I could have," Tina insisted through her tears. "I saw very clearly what a piece of garbage he is! If only

I wouldn't have tried to be nice to him."

"It's the kind of person you are," Hazard insisted. "You want to think the best of everyone. And you don't like to create problems if they can be avoided."

She looked up at him, her brown eyes blurry with tears. He desperately wanted to stop her from hurting, and kissing the hurt away was the only thing he could think of. It wasn't exactly the way his mother used to kiss his cut finger, but the effect was the same. She responded to his kiss in a way that told him she was thinking of something else. And it was obviously the very same thing he was thinking of.

Her arms around his neck were pulling him closer, and the tiny noises that emerged from her throat sent the blood thundering down to his groin.

"You taste nice," she said and then moved her mouth hotly under his, sending him soaring. Their tongues tangled and it didn't take long before he was ready to bring this to the inevitable conclusion.

"Tina?" His voice was a husky groan. "I want you so much."

"Yes," she whispered. "I want you, too."

"Are you sure?" He wanted her to know he wasn't pushing himself onto her.

"I'm sure," she said and ran her hands down his back, down to his buttocks. "But I'm not staying here, you know that."

"That's okay. Let's not think about it." He slid his palms up and down her sides, feeling the svelte body he hungered for so much.

"I feel I'd be using you," she said.

"I doubt very much you're the kind of person who uses anyone," he murmured against her hair. "I think you care for me, just as I care for you. Besides, I think this using can work both ways."

She looked up at him, deep into his eyes. "I do care about you. And that makes this all right? I mean, using you?"

He had to smile at her words. "Yes. Because you care for me, I'm okay with this." Although he wasn't sure he would be okay with loving her and then having her leave.

Because he did love her. There was no doubt in his mind about that. Hadn't been for some time. Probably since he first saw her on the road, waving her red panties. "I don't believe you'd have sex just for your own pleasure. You're the kind of person who has to care about the other person to engage in something that intimate."

She smiled now. "And you're a psychiatrist, too?"

He laughed. "No, but I took a couple of psych. courses in university and—"

"Hi guys, what's up?"

Christopher bounced in through the door and Tina and Hazard flew apart.

She smoothed her hair. "Not much. Hazard was just leaving."

"So were you kissing him good-night?" He removed his sneakers and placed them neatly on the boot tray by the door.

Tina smiled. "Umm . . . yes."

Willing his body to settle down, Hazard grinned at Christopher. "So, what were you guys doing at Florence's?"

Christopher went for the cookie jar on the counter. "May I?" he asked and without waiting for

Tina's okay, he took one of the chocolate chip cookies that he had helped to make. "It was so much fun! We popped popcorn and then threw them in the air and caught them in our mouth."

"Wow! You must have really littered the floor," Tina said. "I hope you helped clean up."

"Nah, didn't have to," Christopher remarked and chewed on his cookie. "They're not fussy like you."

"Really? So you just left the popcorn all over the floor?"

"No, we ate most of them. Didn't wanna waste them. Mutt helped, too."

Tina blanched. "You ate off the floor?"

Hazard grinned, while Christopher headed for the living room. "Yup. And it didn't taste any different. I think we shouldn't throw stuff in the compost just because it falls on the floor. It tastes just the same. I'm gonna watch some TV. That okay?"

"Okay," she said weakly to his back and slapped her forehead, feigning a faint. "Did you hear him? Good Lord! He ate off the floor."

Hazard put a hand on her shoulder. "It won't kill him, you know. Kids aren't that fragile."

"But he's not used to eating germs! In Africa the natives are used to eating things that would kill him. That's the reason I didn't go to Africa to teach, because I was afraid Christopher would catch something deadly."

"He's not in Africa." He could tell she was getting all hyper again about cleanliness. He tried to calm her down, but didn't succeed.

"But things are almost the same here," she insisted.

Hazard felt his anger start to rise. "Look. This is not Africa," he said roughly. "There aren't any scorpions or poisonous snakes here. And there aren't any deadly germs floating around, either. Your precious son is as safe here as he would be in Toronto, or anywhere in Canada."

He hadn't meant to sound defensive, but it was too late to take the angry words back.

There was a glint of defiance in Tina's eyes. "Well, I'm glad you understand that my son is very precious to me," she snapped. "And as his mother I want to protect him from harm as much as humanly possible. Just because you are used to mothers who are drunk most of the day like poor Charlotte's mother, and let their kids get in no end of trouble—"

Hazard turned and headed for the door. "Good night," he said brusquely, and then called out, "Good night, Christopher!"

He wasn't going to hang around and get into a heated argument about the conditions on the reserve. She had no right to paint all the women with the same dirty brush. Most were good, responsible mothers who took care of their children.

But as he angrily strode to his truck a deep feeling of regret filled him. The euphoria brought on by the kisses had as good as evaporated into thin air, replaced by a feeling of hopeless sadness. Maybe she was right and he shouldn't get involved with her. But it was too late for him to turn back from this path, because he couldn't stop himself from loving her.

After Hazard left, Tina sat at the kitchen table chewing on a finger nail. The ragged edge irritated her but she was too upset to walk to the bathroom to get her nail file.

Hazard had walked out on her.

But was it any wonder, after her rude words? How could she have been so insensitive and say such things about the mothers on the rez? No wonder he was angry. He was the chief and it was his duty to protect the people and not let anyone speak ill of them.

Here she had always prided herself on not being prejudiced, and now she'd very plainly shown her true colours. Oh, Lord! She owed him a huge apology. She lowered her head into her arms and her shoulders shook with sobs. They had kissed, and it had been more than wonderful. It had been magical. She had been ready to make love with him, and his body had signaled quite clearly he was on the same page.

But now that he'd seen what an awful hypocrite she was, it would never happen again. He wouldn't want to make love to a woman who despised his people.

But she didn't despise them. She didn't!

Or did she?

Ever since the time she'd seen a woman, obviously very drunk, staggering into the Hudson's Bay store, dragging a tired toddler by the hand, her thoughts about Indigenous women had been less than generous. She had been disgusted and angry, and had voiced her views to Hazard, who had been at the store with her. But, without a word, he had stepped up to the woman and spoken kindly to her. He'd taken the child up in his arms, dirty diaper and all, and had driven the poor woman to a friend's house where she and the child would be taken care of.

He was such a kind man, so gentle, and totally

non-judgmental. If only she could learn to be like that. But she was beginning to realize it wasn't as easy as simply declaring she accepted and tolerated everyone. She just couldn't tolerate that intoxicated mother and what she'd been doing to her toddler. No matter how she tried to get her head around it, she found it totally unacceptable.

The children in her own class she had learned to not only tolerate, but to accept. Even to love. Those dirty hands and fingernails, they didn't bother her. The kids were delightful and funny and so keen to learn. What was there not to love?

Steve's class was less approachable and she mostly stayed away from them while doing recess supervision. As long as their activities weren't breaking the school rules—like smoking, or carrying on behind one of the portables—she preferred to leave them alone. Steve, of course, never came out to supervise, and so Tina was outside every recess to make sure her little ones didn't play rough games and get hurt.

Yes, what would happen to Steve's class now? Since Hazard was going to report him to the authorities first thing tomorrow, Steve wouldn't be around after that. Tina had no doubt that by the afternoon he would be gone, which meant his class would be without a teacher. It wouldn't be easy to get a replacement quickly, so what was Hazard thinking of doing about it?

Somehow Tina already suspected what the answer would be. She would be asked to teach these kids, as well as her own class. She knew that a one-room schoolhouse wasn't uncommon on the smaller First Nation Reserves, but these kids were big and loud and unruly.

Tina shook her head and got up to prepare herself a cup of tea. The wall clock above the sink told her it was almost Christopher's bedtime.

"Do you want some hot chocolate before you go to bed?" she called out but received no answer. She found the boy fully clothed and sound asleep on his bed. Tina smiled. He must have had a rollicking good time next door. As she proceeded to remove his shoes and socks, he made little sleepy noises that went straight to her heart. When had her cute little toddler turned into this gangly boy? A rather unkempt boy who should have had a shower before going to bed. Too late now. Giving him a kiss on the forehead, she pulled the blanket over him and put out the light.

"Good night, honey," she whispered and then returned to the kitchen to tend to the tea kettle that was whistling furiously.

The late autumn night was unusually mild, and Tina brought her teacup out onto the porch. Leaning against the railing, she looked up at the stars that were so visible here. Since her house was at the end of the road, there were no lights to spoil the view of the Great Bear and many other constellations whose names she didn't know. One of them, she remembered from her camping days, was Orion the Hunter, but it was maybe too early in the year for it to appear.

Mutt was sleeping outside his doghouse, keeping guard, and once again Tina was thankful that Hazard had given the dog to Christopher. Loaned it, to be more precise. It made her feel safe to know Mutt would warn her if anything dangerous wandered into the yard.

Just then Mutt sprang up and began to growl.

"What is it, Mutt?" she called to the dog. "Is there another coyote prowling around?"

"No, coyote, just me," came a man's voice from the darkness.

Steve! Tina's heart jumped to her throat.

"What are you doing here?" she asked sharply. "I told you before I don't want you anywhere near me."

"You're sure you don't need some male company?" he asked in a sleazy, thick voice that told her he'd been drinking. He came closer, where the light from the kitchen window shone on him. "I noticed your boyfriend, the Big Chief, just got home a while ago, so I know he's not here any more."

Quickly Tina slipped inside and locked the door behind her. Then, while dialing a number on her phone, she ran to lock the back door and went around slamming shut the bedroom windows she'd opened to let in the night air. In her panic she dialed the only number on the reserve that she knew by heart—Hazard's.

"Please come quickly," she whispered. "Steve is here."

"I'm on my way," Hazard said and hung up.

It wasn't long before his truck pulled into the yard and through the windows Tina saw Hazard circling the house, looking for Steve. A few minutes later he knocked on the door and Tina went to open it.

"I didn't see him, but I didn't expect to," he said and stepped into the kitchen. "I'm sure he took off when he saw my truck."

"I'm so glad you came," Tina said. Would Hazard still be angry with her? He didn't look like he was. Instead his black eyes reflected concern.

"Of course I came," he said and pulled out a chair.

He turned it around and sat on it, legs astride, as usual.

Tina tried not to let her eyes wander to his strong thighs. "Did you talk to him earlier?" she asked. "Is that why he came here, to take revenge on me?"

"I told him the police will be coming to see him in the morning, and he better be at home."

"What about his class?" Tina asked, though she suspected what was coming.

"You think you could look after both classes for a while?" It was a question, not a request. "As a favour to me?" He appealed to her with his dark eyes. How could she say no?

"I . . . I don't know if all the kids will fit into my portable," she tried to reason. "Steve's class has fifteen kids, and they're big."

"I understand it's going to be crowded," Hazard said. "But I'm hoping we can get someone to come and take over very soon."

"How soon?"

"As soon as possible," he said, which told her nothing.

"Sure, I guess I can do it in an emergency," Tina conceded, trying to sound confident. After all what could she say? After the way she'd talked to him she owed him an apology and she hoped he would forgive her. To give herself courage she picked up her cup of cold tea and took a sip.

"Hazard," she began tentatively. "I'm really sorry for what I said earlier about the women here. I don't know what made me say such a horrible thing. Can you forgive me?"

Hazard swung his leg over the chair and came to

stand in front of her. "There's nothing to forgive," he said. "I made you angry and you lashed back at me. I should have known that talking like that to a mother about her son was bound to get a bad reaction. I'm the one who should apologize."

He reached out with one hand to touch her hair, but Tina wished he would reach out with both hands and take her in his arms again.

And then he did. He took the teacup from her and placed it on the counter behind him. Then he pulled her against him and she felt his lips, hot and hungry against her mouth.

"Tina," he groaned, and she slipped her arms round his neck, holding him.

"Oh, Hazard," she whispered. "Hazard."

His hands explored her body and she molded herself against his hardness. He caressed her hips, her narrow waist and moved up to cup her breasts. She unbuttoned her shirt and opened it so he would have better access to them. She wore no bra and his breath caught as her touched her softness.

Please let Christopher stay asleep, she prayed. She wanted Hazard to make love to her. Now. And the thought of being interrupted again was unbearable.

"Do you have a condom?" Tina whispered. "I didn't know I would need to be prepared."

Hazard dug into the back pocket of his jeans. "I'm always prepared," he murmured. "Ever since I've known you, I've been dreaming of it, though not believing it would ever happen."

She led him into her bedroom and locked the door behind them. Unabashed, they undressed in front of each other, and as he divested himself of his jeans and shorts, Tina couldn't take her eyes off his bronzed, smooth body.

Hazard's black eyes glinted with smoldering fires as he looked at her, and Tina knew he loved what he saw.

"You're beautiful," he said in a hoarse whisper.

"You're magnificent," she breathed and swallowed, as desire filled her at the sight of his nakedness.

She lay down on her back on the bed to receive him and he arched his body over her. His lips found hers again. They journeyed down to her throat, and finally to her breasts. His tongue played with each hard nipple and kissed them ardently, while she raised her hips to signal her need.

"Please," she whispered. "Now."

He slid into her and filled her so completely that she moaned in delight. As his long, deep strokes began to have an effect, she gasped and raised herself, tilting her hips to give him better access. She moved in rhythm with his thrusts, which became faster and faster, and her breathing turned to heavy panting. It had been too long since she'd had a man inside her, and never one who completed her so powerfully. She convulsed as the climax racked her body, and as she did she clenched around him and brought him with her in a thunderous orgasm. She bit into his shoulder to keep herself from crying out, and awakening Christopher.

Afterwards they lay side by side on the bed and Hazard stroked her hair gently while their breathing became calm.

Tina caressed his back and smiled with satisfaction. "That was incredibly wonderful," she murmured.

He laughed. "Baby, for me it was beyond wonderful. Beyond incredible."

"I'm expecting Christopher to knock on that door any minute and ask what we guys are doing," she said and reluctantly sat up. "So I think we better not push our luck." She reached for her housecoat on the chair beside the bed.

"You're right." Hazard got up and began to pull on his clothes. "It might require some quick thinking. And I'm too lethargic to think."

It was nice to be together with him again and not be butting heads. She couldn't understand how, when things could be this fabulous, they so often ended up arguing.

But then her mood took a plunge. This all would end soon. And if she was expected to teach Steve's class as well as her own for any length of time, it could all come to a very sudden halt. She had no intention of being driven out of her mind by a bunch of hormonal teenagers.

The truck headlights skimmed the roadside bushes as Hazard drove home along the dark road, feeling mellow and wonderful after the incredible sex. All at once he slammed on the brakes. A man staggered on the side of the road in front of him, and disappeared into the bushes. Even in the dim light, he could tell it was Steve. Hazard grabbed a flashlight out of the glove compartment, jumped out, and shone the beam into the shrubbery that was still moving.

"Come out!" he shouted. "Right now, or I'll send the dogs after you."

The dogs weren't with him, but Steve didn't know

that.

Luckily the bluff worked and Steve crawled out onto the road. He was obviously in a bad way, disheveled and his clothes were awry. What had the man been doing since he ran away from Tina's house, besides drinking some more?

Hazard opened the truck door. "Put your hands behind you," he commanded and groped in the glove compartment for a pair of handcuffs. He slipped them on Steve's wrists and pushed him up into the cab.

"I'm taking you to the police right now," Hazard said and put the truck in gear. "Never mind waiting for them to come for you tomorrow."

By the time he'd explained his mission to the Mounties at the Spruce Falls RCMP Station, and Steve had been booked and locked up, it was almost morning. As Hazard drove home, his mind was preoccupied not only with the horrible actions Steve had committed, but also with Tina.

Neither brought him any peace of mind.

Chapter Ten

Tina stood at her portable door the following morning, waiting for the kids to arrive. Her heart was fluttering up in her throat and she hoped it wouldn't prevent her from speaking with authority. She had moved the little desks along one wall and placed them into groups of four to make room for the big desks that would be carried in by the kids themselves. She had also brought all the books she could find from their classroom and placed them on the window ledge. There were so few of them, and they were in such poor condition, that she made a mental note to order more the first chance she had.

Little by little the kids streamed into the yard, playing on the swings and hanging around in groups till she rang the bell. Steve's class lined up outside their portable and, with legs that felt like limp spaghetti, Tina walked over to address them. Briefly she told them their teacher had left and asked them to help each other carry the desks and chairs into her portable.

She looked at Charlotte who smiled at her shyly and then quickly lowered her eyes before the others saw the exchange. This gave her courage to tackle the difficult task ahead and with a nod of determination she went to look after her own pupils, who were lined up behind their door looking on with curiosity at what was going on next door.

The move didn't take long. With a tremendous amount of noise and confusion the desks were brought in and placed where Tina indicated. Then the children all settled down and challenged her with their eyes to make her next move.

"We'll stand up to sing 'O Canada'," Tina said, trying to make her voice carry authority. It was how she always started the day, but it was obviously not what the older kids had done. Grinning at each other they slowly stood up and leaned against their desks while the little ones began to sing with gusto. As the song progressed, several of the younger pupils looked at the slouching older kids and slowly most of them stopped singing. Tina sang to the end along with just a few of her kids, despite wanting to throw in the towel right then and there. Why was she even bothering? It wasn't going to work.

After everyone had sat down with clatter and scraping of chairs, Tina tacked up a large sheet of paper on the board.

"I have written out the words for 'O Canada' in the Ojibwa language, and we'll all learn it," she told the big kids. She was gratified to see a glint of interest in many of their eyes.

She sang the first line: "O Canada! Omaa-Saa-Wen Gee Yang. Now sing it with me."

And surprise of surprises, most of them hesitantly joined her.

"Tomorrow we'll learn the second line, and each day we'll learn one more, until we know how to sing it all in Ojibwa," Tina said. "Now you will write it down in your Ojibwa language books."

"Huh? Language books?" she heard murmurs. "What language books?"

She handed out a pile of workbooks to one of the boys. "Please hand these out to your group as well as the grade threes. These are your Ojibwa language books. We'll be writing down the words of several songs in them."

"Like 'Rock-a-baby Rock'?" one of the boys asked with an obvious attempt at intimidation.

"No, not that one," Tina replied calmly. "Unless you know it in Ojibwa? No? We'll write down the words of songs that I have found in the Ojibwa language. This morning, after you have written 'O Canada', you'll memorize the first line for tomorrow. Then you will take out your crayons and—"

"Crayons?" one boy snickered. "Oh, yeah, our crayons."

"We don't got no crayons!" others called out to general laughter.

"I'll get each of you a box after lunch, but for now you may borrow the crayons from that lost crayon box on the window ledge. I want you to decorate the cover of your language books with something that shows your pride in your Indigenous heritage. I'm sure you can think of something much better than I can. And please feel free to chat quietly among yourselves if you need ideas. And I stress the word quietly, because in the meanwhile I'll be doing number work with the grade ones and twos. If you are finished before I get back to you, take out a book and read. Quietly. There are some books on the window ledge."

Mentally she crossed her fingers and went to sit with the group of ones and twos—including Christopher. To her surprise most of the big kids settled down to work and started to write down the song. Then they began to decorate the covers, sharing their ideas in low murmurs.

Tina sighed with relief. Maybe this would work after all, even with a crowded classroom.

When the ones and twos had been assigned their seatwork, she moved on to teach the grade threes, and then, group by group she worked through math lessons for each grade level of the junior and intermediate kids. After Hazard had left last night—she could still feel the delicious effects of their lovemaking inside her body—she had stayed up till wee hours getting the lessons and seatwork ready.

At recess she stood outside and chatted with some of the older kids, which was something she hadn't done up till now. Why had she been so intimidated by them? They were just kids, after all, and eager to share their experiences when asked by a concerned, interested adult.

Yes, she would definitely stay till Christmas if things continued like today. After all, what was the hurry? Thinking about last night with Hazard she didn't feel she needed—or wanted—to make a quick exit.

And now that the whole school was in her hands, how could she possibly abandon these children?

The obvious answer was, she couldn't.

Hazard dropped by her portable after the children

had left. He knocked on the door and Christopher ran to meet him. Tina continued to mark the stack of papers on her desk and only smiled her greeting.

"Hi, Hazard!" the boy called with great excitement. "We had some big kids in our class today and they're coming again tomorrow."

"No kidding?" Hazard said. "So, how was it?"

Tina knew the questing was meant for her, but she had to agree with the reply Christopher gave.

"Really good," the boy reported proudly.

"Yeah?" Hazard came over to her desk and now aimed the question directly at her. "It really was good?"

"Mommy, I've done my number work," Christopher called. "I'm going out to swing, okay?" And off he ran without waiting for a reply.

Tina put her pencil down and looked up at Hazard who settled his hip on the corner of the desk. "It went really well, like Christopher told you. After being almost sick to my stomach with fear in the morning, I must say I was pleasantly surprised."

Hazard laughed with relief. "Whew! I was scared all day that you'd jump in your car and drive off. I even regretted letting George borrow my truck to take you to Big Thunder and buy that car."

Tina smiled at him. It was wonderful just to have him so close. "Well, not today," she said. "But maybe tomorrow."

Hazard reached to grip her shoulder. "Please, don't say that. I don't know what I'd do."

The memories of last night flooded back and Tina tilted her head to lay a cheek against his hand. He bent down to kiss the top of her head.

"I mean without a teacher in the school." He stood

up and his other hand slid down her back to caress her warmly. "Or without you."

Tina shook her head. "Hazard, I told you I don't want you to—"

"I know. I know. You don't want me to get hurt. I had a helluva time getting to sleep last night. And not just because of that lout, Steve. I wanted you there beside me and couldn't sleep because you weren't."

"Hazard, please stop! Please don't say anything!" Tina cried.

But despite her words, he persisted. "I'm afraid it's too late. When you go—"

"Hazard, I told you right from the get-go that I wasn't going to stay here." Oh, Lord, this was getting too difficult, because something told her that when she left, it wouldn't be just he who would be hurting.

"Yes, you did say that. And I keep telling myself that all the time. Every day, and especially every night. But somehow I still come to the same conclusion."

"Which is?" Why did she ask, when she didn't want to hear it? When she already knew what he would say.

"That I love you. I don't have any right to ask you to stay, and I'm not going to. But I want to say it to you, and, dammit all, I don't want you to leave."

"Oh God! that's not fair."

She'd been praying this word would never come up between them, because she didn't want to deal with such emotions. Fighting to keep her voice from shaking, she turned to face him. "Hazard, you can't say that."

"I know. But I just did. That was damned stupid of me, so just pretend it didn't happen, okay?"

"Last night was wonderful," she said evenly. "But

I'm not going to stay here. I have a condo in Toronto, as well as my parents and lots of very good friends waiting for me to come back home. I don't belong here."

"No, you don't. So why did you come in the first place?" Hazard's voice was dark, almost threatening.

"I came because I wanted to do something meaningful with my life. I knew there was a scarcity of teachers in the north and so I—"

"Meaningful? That's an interesting word." He sounded sarcastic. "Like you came here with the idea of fixing things for all us poor, ignorant Indians?"

"That is not what I mean!" Tina cried. "It's not the same thing at all. You are making me sound like some kind of a do-gooder. I'm not! I told you if I didn't have Christopher, I would have gone to Africa to help out there."

"I wish the hell you had!" Hazard spat out, turned on his heel and walked out.

He sat in his truck without turning on the engine. Gritting his teeth, he whacked the steering wheel in fury.

He couldn't believe what he'd just said. Why the hell couldn't he have kept his mouth shut and just enjoyed her company. Enjoyed making love to her, instead of blurting out that he loved her? But it was obvious she had no such thoughts, and last night hadn't meant the same for her as it had to him. Sure, she said it had been wonderful, but what she'd meant was that she'd liked the sex. And what was there not to like? He was more than adequate as a lover, and he knew that. But her tone of voice and especially her words had conveyed loudly that good sex wasn't enough of a draw for her. Her condo in Toronto and her very good friends—Hazard's lip curled in angry disdain—meant more to her than whatever he could offer.

He turned on the ignition. But at least she hadn't minced her words. He had to give her that. She'd given it to him straight and he had to admire her honesty. He put the truck in gear and the tires squealed as he tore out of the schoolyard. That was the last time he would go to her house. He didn't need sex that badly. There were others.

Others, whom he didn't want.

He sighed. He didn't make love to Tina because he needed sex. He made love to her because he loved her. It was she who obviously wanted sex and had used him for this purpose. She'd as good as told him that.

By the time he reached his house he was calmer and had come to a decision. He accepted that he was powerless to prevent her from leaving at the end of the school year. Maybe even sooner. He also knew he would be left missing her. But in the meanwhile he was going take whatever she was willing to offer. And why not? He knew he was happier with her, than without. The hell with logic. He was bound to see her all the time in town, and it would be unbearable to have her so near and not be with her. So why not just continue this charade?

Except . . . Hazard groaned. What had he said to her as he left? That he wished the hell she had gone to Africa! Damn! Now how would she receive him when they met? Probably with a very cold shoulder. And rightfully so.

Well, there was nothing he could do about it tonight. Hazard opened the door of his house and

entered the dark kitchen. Not even the furious wagging of Jeff's tail cheered him up. Despondently he
reached into the fridge for a can of beer and pulled
open the tab. Taking a huge gulp he slumped down
into an armchair to stare at the dark TV.

Tina was surprised how cooperative the bigger kids
were when they were in the same class with the little
ones. Perhaps it was because many of the youngsters
in the lower grades were their sisters and brothers,
and they didn't want to show bad behavior in front of
them. They read to the kindergartens and grade ones,
and helped the grade twos and threes with their math.
They all had physical education together, and when
they played baseball in the yard they coached the little
ones when it was their turn at bat. After school they
put up art on the bulletin boards and even marked
some of the easier assignments, saving Tina hours of
work. Of course she had to prepare eight sets of lessons and make up assignments for every grade level,
but day by day this task became less and less onerous,
as she became familiar with the curriculum.

As the weeks passed, she kept an eye on Charlotte,
whose pregnancy was beginning to show. Hazard had
driven with the girl to Spruce Falls to have the doctor
check her out and give her an ultrasound. Everything
was progressing normally. Tina had hoped that when
Charlotte saw her baby's ultrasound picture, she
would start to think about keeping it, but no such
luck. Several times since then, Charlotte had mentioned about giving the baby to Tina, who didn't have
the heart to tell her she couldn't possibly take the baby
with her when she left. Not being sure how fragile

Charlotte's emotional state was, she didn't want to say anything that would upset her at this point.

Of course her own emotions were in a complete turmoil. Since Hazard had told her he loved her, and then had wished her off to the farthest corner of Africa, they'd only had a few polite and very strained conversations. His words had put a stop to their lovemaking—not that they would've had many opportunities for such activities, anyway—and he no longer dropped by the house or popped into her classroom after school. He was polite, but restrained, and this nearly drove her mad.

As the days passed and their relationship showed no signs of improving, Tina decided it was time for her to speak up. She missed his kisses and his company, but it didn't look like he was going to be the one to say anything. It was obvious his pride was hurt. After he had confessed his love, her apparent brush-off had probably been too much for him to swallow. Could she blame him?

One Friday after school, she left Christopher to play with James and Chogan and then, with a feeling of trepidation, drove up to Hazard's house.

When he answered her knock, his eyes flew open in surprise.

"Hi," she said. "May I come in?"

She saw him hesitate and immediately felt like a fool. Why had she come? What could she say that would make any difference? She couldn't very well apologize for saying the truth about leaving.

"Sure," he then said and stepped aside to let her come in.

Tina sighed with relief, but when she entered, she

stopped and stared at the packs of supplies on the floor. It was obvious he was getting ready to go somewhere.

"You're going on a trip or something?" she asked.

His reply was laconic. "Yeah. I'm going with a bunch of guys on a moose hunt. Leaving tomorrow morning."

"Oh." Now Tina really felt like a fool. No way could she stay and start to talk about emotional stuff when the man was getting ready to leave on a hunting trip. She knew instinctively the two weren't exactly compatible topics, but she couldn't just turn around and leave without saying something.

"So how long will you be away?" she asked.

"A couple of weeks," Hazard told her, sending her heart plummeting to her toes.

"Oh." Two weeks. Fourteen more days and nights of missing him. How could she bear it?

He stood before her, arms crossed across his chest. "So, what can I do for you?" he asked.

It was obvious he was uncomfortable with her presence and probably wished she would get the hell out of Dodge and let him go on with his preparations.

"Oh, nothing much," she said, keeping her voice casual. "Just thought I'd drop by to see what you're up to. I haven't seen very much of you lately, and—"

Hazard's eyes were inscrutable. "Why? Have you missed me?"

Tina wasn't sure if he was being funny or serious, and decided to play funny. "Missed you? You bet! Just like the black flies."

Hazard didn't laugh. She'd played the wrong card. He was serious.

"Well, at the risk of being slapped down, I'll confess I've missed you," he said. His eyes looked into hers and she was afraid she might drown in them.

"Why would I slap you down?" She had to whisper, for no sound came out of her throat.

He came closer. Close enough that she could smell the masculine scent of him. And then, inexplicably, she found herself in his arms. He was holding her tightly against him, whispering her name into her hair, and making her heart pound with happiness.

"Hazard," she murmured. "I've missed you so much."

He groaned. "And here I have to leave, just when I found you again." He kissed her, and she opened her mouth to him, clinging to him, not able to get enough of his nearness.

"Please just hold me," Tina whimpered. "Don't say anything about leaving just now! I need you so."

"Oh, baby, I thought I'd go mad when I thought you'd never forgive me for what I said to you. I was so angry, the words just came out."

She stroked his cheek. "It's all right, I've already forgotten what you said." Then she added with a wicked grin, "But whatever it was—like I always say to the kids—don't do it again."

"Stop being a teacher for once," Hazard rumbled. "I have to make this last for two long weeks." And again he pressed his lips on hers, making her head swim.

"I won't keep you from your preparations," she murmured and made to get out of his arms, but he picked her up.

"My preparations can wait," he said. "This can't." And he laughed triumphantly as he kicked open the bedroom door.

"I've been thinking," Tina said and put down her marking pencil on the kitchen table. Although they'd only just finished dinner, the late November evening was already dark. Light from the windows fell on the snow, creating shadows of trees on the whiteness. Hazard was lounging on the couch, watching TV while by his feet Christopher played a computer game on his iPod.

"Thinking? Hope it didn't hurt."

Christopher giggled at Hazard's joke.

Tina ignored them. "I've been thinking that I'd like to ask George to give the bigger kids lessons on how to do wood carvings. It could be part of the art classes."

"Sounds good to me, as long as George is willing," Hazard said.

"I'll ask him." This was great. Hazard hadn't put up any roadblocks. She never knew how he would react to her suggestions concerning "his people".

For a few minutes there was silence as Tina continued her marking. Should she try and see how her next idea would be received?

"And I could ask Harold if he would give lessons to some of the older kids on how to make moccasins. It would be a shame to have that art die with him."

"Yeah. He could probably do that."

Now for the next idea, while he was almost in a state of stupor.

"I was also thinking that after Christmas I could help organize night classes where Anna could show the women how to bake bread. A big bag of flour is a lot cheaper than buying loaves of bread."

Hazard yawned. He looked ready to doze off. "Sounds good to me."

He stretched out his long legs on the couch while Tina pressed on. "Harold also makes lovely buckskin jackets. Have you seen them?"

"Of course. I have one myself." He yawned again. "I believe his cousin, Susan, decorates them with quills and beads. She's good."

"Yes, you're right." It was good that the idea came from him. "Susan could give the kids classes on bead-work and quills. Fabulous! That's pretty well the whole junior and intermediate art program ready for the next term."

Hazard sat up and grinned. "Right. You expect me to believe you hadn't thought of Susan. I'll bet you have a job for every person on the reserve."

Tina went over and gave him a knuckle sandwich. She would rather have kissed him, but not in front of Christopher.

Hazard grabbed her wrist and pulled her down on top of him.

Christopher dropped his iPod on the rug and joined the game by jumping on top of her. "Mom, you're our prisoner!" he sang.

"That's right, you're my prisoner and I'll never let you go," Hazard added, making her heart jump up to her throat where its rapid beating left her breathless.

"You can't say that," she whispered. "It's not right."

"But it's true, it's true," he sang, mimicking Christopher, although his dark eyes, piercing into hers were anything but playful.

"Mom's my prisoner, too," Christopher pressed his knobby knees against her back. "And she's never gonna be free. Ever."

"Ouch, you're hurting me," Tina cried. "Let me go, you idiots. Both of you."

"No, no, never," Christopher sang. "Never, never, never!"

"Never," Hazard echoed, and pulled her face down against his. The kiss was quick, but he used the few seconds skillfully, making her gasp.

"Don't," she hissed when her mouth was free to speak. "Let me go."

"Are you saying 'Don't let me go,' or 'Don't, exclamation point, let me go, exclamation point'?" Hazard asked. But he relaxed his hold on her as she dug her fingers into his chest, scowling menacingly. "Obviously she means the latter. We have to release our prisoner," Hazard said to Christopher. "She's getting vicious."

When she was free, Tina sprang up, brushed the hair off her face with her fingers and turned her back on them. "You two are impossible." She marched to the table and picked up her marking pencil, but it took a while before her heart had settled down and she could concentrate on the math problems.

As December drew near, Tina spent her evenings planning a program for the Christmas concert and learning some Christmas songs in the Ojibwa language. She had asked around the village for someone who would be good for teaching the children the correct pronunciation. To her surprise, many people recommended Alice Long Feather, Charlotte's mother. Apparently she had a lovely singing voice and was quite fluent in Ojibwa.

So every morning Alice came to the school—totally

sober—and sang for an hour with the students while Tina sat at her desk listening and tried to mouth the words. She had no idea what Alice did during then rest of the day, but it was wonderful to see her so committed to this activity, and putting forth such an effort. It was also a great revelation to Charlotte, who knew her mother could sing, but hadn't believed her capable of teaching songs to a classroom full of kids.

Tina found the language very difficult to learn, but most of the children seemed to pick up the words quite readily. Even if they didn't speak it themselves, they'd been exposed to the Ojibwa language all their lives. By now they had already learned "O Canada" in Ojibwa by heart, and Tina was happy that even the most surly boys sang it with pride every morning.

She had been teaching them about their culture and each day she read them an Ojibwa legend in English, which the pupils then illustrated. She planned to bind these stories and pictures into a booklet for the almost non-existent school library. The lack of books concerned her, and she had brought many of Christopher's books from home to supplement the primary book shelf. The children asked her almost daily about the parcel they were expecting from the supplier from whom Tina had ordered books for the older students.

She no longer spoke about leaving at Christmas. There was just too much to do with tests, report cards and decorations. And Charlotte leaned on her more and more as the pregnancy progressed, asking probing questions about her body. She was very curious about the impending birth, often staying after school to talk about the birthing process.

"Will it hurt very much?" Charlotte now asked as

Karen Rossi

she sat at a desk, cutting up stars from tin foil and taping them onto a string. "How long will it take?"

The afternoon sky had already darkened and at four-thirty the twilight had arrived. It would have been darker, except for the snow that brightened up the night.

Tina had climbed up a ladder to hang up the strings of stars to run from one ceiling fixture to another. Rather than staying around after school with Tina, Christopher had walked home with James and Chogan, so they could have more time to play outside in the long twilight. Florence had always offered to look after Christopher when he was playing with her sons.

"I'm afraid I can't say anything about the pain," Tina said to Charlotte from her perch. "Every woman is different. Some have their baby in a just an hour or two, while others have a longer labor. And the pain varies, too. But I can say for certain it will hurt at least a bit. I hope not too much. Please hand me another string, Charlotte."

"How was it for you?" Charlotte wanted to know as she reached up to give Tina the stars.

"I had quite a bit of pain but my labor was only about six hours."

"Six hours!" Charlotte yelped. "I don't want to be hurting for six hours."

"Don't worry. They give you stuff for the pain," Tina reassured her and then tried to distract her from any more questions about pain. "Could you hand me the roll of tape, please?"

And to Tina's relief, as they hung up the Christmas decorations around the classroom, Charlotte forgot about the ordeal that awaited her in the spring. Instead she surprised Tina by offering such good decorating ideas, that it was obvious the girl had an artistic eye. Perhaps one day she might earn a living doing something with this gift. Tina would certainly try to encourage her in that direction.

What was she thinking? She wouldn't be here to encourage anyone. Charlotte would graduate from grade eight in June, the mother of an infant, and Tina would fly back home. End of story. But she tried not to let the thought get her down as she continued to tidy up after Charlotte left.

There was stomping at the portable door and Hazard stepped in, first knocking the snow off his boots. He'd taken to dropping by the school whenever he could, and Tina was always glad when Christopher wasn't there. It gave them a few precious moments together. For kissing. And cuddling. She always tried to not let the knowledge of her leaving spoil their moments together, and put those thoughts onto the back-burner of her mind.

Since his return from a very successful moose hunting trip they'd had no arguments, thank goodness. The moose meat had been divided up between several families and Tina, also, had received her share.

"Hazard," she now asked, after he'd thoroughly kissed her. "Can you tell me what moose organ is long and thick? Last night I opened up a package of frozen meat and discovered a very strange-looking chunk."

Hazard cocked an eyebrow and gave her a mischievous look. "Well . . ."

Tina slapped his chest. "I'm sure it's not what you're thinking, unless someone played a very crude joke on me."

He laughed. "Okay, I'm sure it's not that. If it has lots of little bumps on it, it could be the tongue."

"The tongue? Yuck!" Tina cried, sticking out her own. "When I get home, I am going to throw that horrible thing out for the coyotes."

"Oh, no, don't do that. No feeding the wildlife, remember? Besides, it's delicious."

"It's my horrible thing to dispose of as I please," she insisted.

"Then please dispose of it in my direction," Hazard said. "I'll cook it up and then you can have a taste."

"You can have it but I'll not take a bite!" she declared hotly, putting an end to any discussion about moose tongues.

But she was much more agreeable to loving. Hazard's hands caressed her until she was ready to ask him to hoist her onto the teacher's desk and make love to her right there.

"When will Christopher be away?" he growled, his black eyes glistening with passion.

"Nothing's been planned," Tina replied. Her heart hammered and desire filled her.

"Please plan something. Soon." Hazard nuzzled her neck and sent sweet shivers down her spine.

She threw back her head to give him access to her throat. "Yes, I will," she whispered. "Soon."

Chapter Eleven

But any such plans were pushed aside, because when Tina got home, Christopher met her in the yard, bursting with excitement.

"Nana called!" he cried. "We talked a long time and then she told you to call her back."

"What were you doing inside the house on your own?" Tina asked severely. "You know you're not supposed to—"

"I had to pee," Christopher interrupted. "It's too cold to pee against a tree."

Tina laughed. He had a point there. But she knew what her mother's first words would be when she called.

"Dear," her mother began without even saying hello. "Why was Christopher at home alone?"

Damn! Of course he would have been inside just when the phone call came. While Tina was at school making out with the chief.

"He just came in to use the washroom, Mom," Tina told her, not wanting to start defending herself or explaining things. "He was playing outside. He has a babysitter."

"Well, not a very responsible one, it seems to me," Mrs. Lawrence's voice was heavy with censure.

Tina grimaced. "Mom, I'm sure you didn't call to check up on Christopher's babysitter," she said, making an effort to sound civil. "What's up?"

"Well, Daddy and I have a surprise for you." Mrs. Lawrence's voice now was filled with excitement. "Since you won't come home for Christmas, we've decided to come and visit you. Christmas wouldn't be Christmas if we weren't with our only daughter and grandchild." Now tears coloured her voice.

Oh, oh! A wave of panic swept through Tina. "Of course! And I want to spend Christmas with my only Mom and Dad." It wasn't as though she didn't want them here, but . . . "Are you sure you want to come in the winter? It's quite cold, you know. Only five degrees here today."

"It's not exactly balmy here in Toronto, either," her mother informed her rather smartly.

"But we have lots of snow," Tina tried again.

Obviously her mother wasn't going to be scared off by that. "Daddy and I both have winter boots, dear. You're starting to sound like you don't want us to come."

"Oh, Mom, of course I want you to come!" Tina exclaimed, crossing her fingers behind her back. "It's just that it's such a long and arduous trip."

"Dear, it can't be as bad as when we were on our Antarctica cruise."

That put an end to Tina's objections. Of course the trip to Antarctica had been on a well-serviced luxury liner and her parents hadn't had much else to do but enjoy themselves. But Tina knew in her mother's books that was now the measuring stick for anything that winter could dish out. Nothing could ever come close to the Antarctica experience.

"We'll book a flight to Big Thunder," Mrs. Lawrence said. "Can you come and pick us up from there? Daddy doesn't want to rent a car and drive in wintry conditions."

"I'm very glad Daddy's decided not to drive. But Big Thunder is pretty far for me to pick you up. You'll have to take a bus from Big Thunder to Spruce Falls. I'll pick you up from there in my car."

"That's fine, we'll do that. But please don't tell Christopher. Part of his Christmas gift is a surprise visit from his Nana and Papa." Mrs. Lawrence giggled in anticipation.

After hanging up Tina sat at the kitchen table for a few minutes digesting the situation. Where could her parents stay? She got up to make herself a cup of coffee and then sat down again to think about it. How would it all work out? The only inn at the rez wasn't exactly a five-star hotel, and the one in Spruce Falls was too far away. So the only choice was for her parents to stay in this little house. They could sleep in her bedroom, while she moved into Christopher's room. He in turn, would have to sleep on the couch in the living room.

The back screen door banged and Christopher ran in. "Can I have a cookie, Mom?" he yelled.

Tina had noted that for some time he'd no longer called her Mommy, and the thought made her feel somewhat nostalgic. Her little boy was growing up.

"Don't bring all that snow in," Tina reminded him for the umpteenth time. "Go back and brush off your snowsuit on the steps. And knock the snow off your boots before you put them on the boot tray.

A few moments later, having shed his outdoor gear, he ran into the kitchen and took the top off the cookie jar.

"Wash your hands first." He still had to be reminded, after six years of nagging.

Christopher ran cold water over his fingers. "Did you call Nana?" He wiped his hands on the terry towel hanging on a doorknob, and reached deep into the cookie jar.

"I did, and we had a very good conversation," Tina told him. Luckily he didn't ask for further details. "One cookie will do. Dinner will be ready soon."

As she pulled a pot of stew from the fridge and placed it on the stove to heat, her mind kept circling around the forthcoming visit. Mom and Dad would definitely have a hard time fitting into the reserve scene and dealing with Tina's new friends. Hazard—she didn't even want to think about that right now. He was more than a friend, and she was afraid this would show in her behavior toward him. Maybe it was best if he didn't come around while her parents were here.

Tina chewed on one of her nails as she stirred the pot. God, that didn't seem right. What would Hazard think of that? How would he react? Better not think about that now or she would become totally depressed.

And what would her parents say about Charlotte and her condition? Although in that instance Tina could always remind them of her own pregnancy. And what about Christopher's best friends, James and Chogan, whose personal hygiene wasn't exactly exemplary?

Tina grimaced. Nowadays Christopher was even

less mindful about washing his hands than before, and with all his outdoor activities there was always dirt under his nails. And Tina usually forgot to clean them. What would Mom say about that? And often he was two or three weeks—sometimes even more—behind with his haircuts. Which wasn't his fault, of course, but Tina's own negligence. But all this didn't seem to have hurt him. In fact—she smiled to herself as she stirred the pot—the shaggy hair made him look kind of cute. He'd been talking about growing his hair long, like Hazard's, and tying it up into a pony tail. Yeah, like that would go over big with Nana and Papa.

But one good thing was that so far he hadn't been sick, not even a day. Tina found herself more relaxed about the health rules she'd conscientiously followed ever since he was born, a sickly, underweight infant.

After dinner Tina sat in the living room, staring with unseeing eyes at the TV screen while Christopher lay on his stomach at her feet, playing with his iPod. What would it be like with her parents staying in this house which had only one bathroom? She had bitten her tongue and not asked how long they would stay, because she knew her mother would have considered that the epitome of bad manners. But Tina wished Mom had given her at least some idea. All she could hope for was that they would come just before Christmas and go back home for their traditional New Year's celebrations at the Country Club. A week of juggling showers they could maybe deal with. Maybe.

She felt like such a disloyal daughter. She loved her parents and owed them so much. But this was going to be very difficult.

And what about Hazard?

The notes of "Jingle Bells" rang through the Greenstone Community Centre, where the junior and intermediate students stood on the stage, singing, while the grade ones and twos, sitting cross-legged in front of them, jingled their bells enthusiastically. After the applause had died Tina signaled for Charlotte to announce the next performance and a few moments later the kindergarten children joined them on stage. They were wearing white shepherd robes and carrying little drums, which the bigger students had made for them. While the choir sang the song, the little drummers charmed the audience by simply standing there, beating their drums off-rhythm.

Several other performances followed, including more songs and a poem. One of the grade eight boys read a short story in the Ojibwa language in a deep, mature voice, while beside him a girl repeated it in English.

At the end of the evening the whole school stood on stage to sing "Silent Night" in Ojibwa, while Tina conducted them from the piano.

"Gichitwaa-dibikad," they sang, and finished off with, "Christ sa gii-niigid! Christ sa gii-niigid!"

It almost made Tina's eyes fill to see them all, from the oldest grade eight boy to the youngest kindergarten child, singing with such obvious pride. When the song ended and the enthusiastic applause had died down, Charlotte brought out an A-frame with the words of the first verse of "Silent Night" written in large print in Ojibwa, and invited everyone to sing along while the choir repeated the song.

Tina brought the concert to a close by asking everyone to enjoy the treats laid out on tables along the walls, courtesy of the parents and grandparents. As she mingled with the audience, carrying her plate of goodies, she was congratulated and praised until she started to feel embarrassed. She'd only done what any teacher would do at Christmas time, but it seemed the Christmas concert was the first one this school community had enjoyed for years, and so it generated great excitement.

Hazard came and stood by her side, a plate of sandwiches in his hand. "How does it feel to be the celebrity of Greenstone?" he asked.

Tina grinned. She knew her face was flushed, partly from the heat generated in the Community Centre by the many bodies, and partly from exhilaration.

"It feels good," she said. "But all this praise is totally overblown," she added modestly.

"Just enjoy it. You deserve the praise. The kids are so proud of their accomplishments."

Tina looked around the large, pine-paneled room where the smallest children were running around with abandon. Now that her role in the evening's activities was done, she'd decided to leave the disciplining to the parents. Everyone was happy enjoying themselves, which was the point of the whole event.

Hazard laid his empty paper plate on one of the long tables, covered by white paper tablecloths. "So, your parents are coming soon?"

"Yes, Christopher and I'll drive to Spruce Falls day after tomorrow to pick them up."

Hazard nodded, smiling. "Right. You must be getting pretty excited."

Tina grimaced. "Nervous would better describe it. I have no idea how they'll react to all this." She waved a hand around the room.

His smile died and was replaced by a puzzled frown. "What's to react? It's a kids' party."

Tina hesitated. "I mean the . . . people," she said cautiously. Too cautiously. "They're different from what my folks are used to." She suspected he wouldn't take her words sitting down. He didn't. As she'd feared, Hazard's jaw stiffened and his back straightened visibly.

"Yeah, they're not fancy and refined like the upper-crusty types your parents are used to dealing with." He didn't even try to hide his sarcasm.

No use trying to deny it. "No, they're not," Tina said. "Mom and Dad are used to a very different crowd." Although he already knew all this, she wanted to stress the reality, and try to make him see the difficult situation in which this visit placed her. What was worse, she still hadn't figured out how to tell him he should keep a low profile while her parents were here. "They live in big houses and drive big cars. Some have chauffeurs and gardeners," she said.

Hazard snorted. "These people here probably wouldn't even get hired as kitchen help."

After a moment of silence, during which Tina desperately tried to find a way to avoid replying, she simply admitted, "Probably not."

Hazard's eyes were inscrutable as he looked at her for a few moments. "I guess you'd be more comfortable if I didn't add to their culture shock by dropping in during their visit?"

Tina blushed. He had just saved her from the embarrassment of telling him that. But it was not for the reason he thought. If he came by, she was sure her parents would be astute enough to see that she and Hazard had something happening between them. Their eyes, as they looked at each other, would be a sure give-away. She could only imagine her parents' reaction. Her father would cough discreetly, and her mother would ask, very cautiously, "But you're not in love with him, are you, dear?" And she would say, "Of course not." Because that she wasn't.

Was she?

All this went through her mind while he stood waiting for her answer. Which never came.

Obviously he understand that her silence was her reply. "Well, maybe I'll see you around," he said and turned to go.

Torn by guilt, she let it happen, although her heart screamed for him to come back.

Tina's nerves were on edge during the whole trip to Spruce Falls and back, preparing for the moment when she would steer the car into her driveway. She'd tried to imagine how the little clapboard house might appear to her mother. Fortunately it was late in the afternoon and the sun had set by the time they got to Greenstone, so in the twilight Mrs. Lawrence couldn't get a very good view of the reserve. She sat in the back with Christopher, her neck craned, trying to see into the dusky evening. Tina was glad a blanket of snow covered the yards, which looked much tidier than they had appeared to her when she had arrived in the summer.

She pulled up in front of her home. "Oh, what a cute little house!" Mrs. Lawrence cried when she got out of the car. But the lack of delight in her voice conflicted with her words. "You sent me photos of it, but this is so . . . so different."

Her father only harrumphed lightly, which—Tina knew—was his way of avoiding having to express a negative opinion. But their reactions sent her into a defensive mode.

"I told you many times it's small. It only has two bedrooms and one bathroom." She was sure her mother still hadn't grasped the impact this fact would have on her during the visit.

They walked to the house along the path Christopher had shoveled in the morning. Tina lugged one heavy suitcase, while Mr. Lawrence carried the other, and Christopher helpfully carried his Nana's overnight case. Mrs. Lawrence carried two large shopping bags from expensive department stores which, Tina suspected, were their Christmas gifts.

Christopher opened the door and politely let his grandmother enter first.

"Yes, it is a cute little house," Mrs. Lawrence reiterated as she stepped into the tiny porch. "Very little." She stood facing the narrow hallway, while everyone else waited outside behind her, unable to pass.

"Excuse me, Mom, but we're all standing out here in the cold. Please go in further," Tina urged, trying to contain her impatience. The suitcase weighed at least half a ton and her fingers were getting numb, gripping the handle.

Mrs. Lawrence moved against the hall wall, trying to make herself smaller. "Maybe you can show me around the house so I'll know where I should go."

"Well, you're looking at just about the whole place right now." Tina squeezed by her and deposited the suitcase on the living room floor with a heavy thump. "This is the living room. You can go and sit on the couch and rest your tired feet."

"My feet are not tired. I've been sitting all day." There was an edge in Mrs. Lawrence's voice.

Tina gritted her teeth, trying to remain calm. Of course Mom was not impressed by what she saw.

"Nana, your bedroom is just down the hall," Christopher piped up. "Yours and Papa's. Come on. I'll show you." He dropped the overnight bag on the living room floor and grabbed his grandparents by the hand, leading them into Tina's bedroom.

Tina joined them, standing at the bedroom door. The little room was too crowded for her to enter.

"You and Papa sleep here," Christopher announced. Tina was surprised by the pride in his voice. He sounded like an innkeeper, showing off his best luxury suite.

"Both of us? On that bed?"

The horror in her mother's voice was obvious to everyone but Christopher. "Yep. It's for both of you," he said proudly.

"I think we can fit on a double bed, dear," Mr. Lawrence said, chuckling. "It will be very cozy."

Tina smiled as her mother, a small, pleasantly plump woman, pulled in her stomach and muttered, "Yes, well, I don't know . . ."

Her tall Dad had a good-sized belly, and the thought of them sharing the double bed made Tina shake her head. Mom was right to be horrified.

"It's Mom's bed, but she'll sleep in my room while you're here," Christopher explained.

"And you?"

Tina detected a slight tremor in her mother's voice and felt some sympathy. This was probably quite a jarring experience for her. Her only daughter and grandson lived in "these conditions".

"I'm sleeping in the living room," Christopher blithely went on. "On the couch." He hadn't the slightest idea how all this looked to his grandparents. "But that means you guys can't make too much noise in the morning. I don't have to go to school 'cause it's Christmas holidays, and I want to sleep in every morning."

"Of course, dear," Mrs. Lawrence said feebly.

"This is the bathroom." Christopher opened the door to the tiny washroom at the end of the hall. "We're all sharing it, so we have to take turns brushing our teeth and stuff."

"The bathroom?"

"Mom," Tina said impatiently. "I told you there's just one bathroom. I told you many times."

"But if Grandpa's in a hurry, he can go outside and pee against a tree," Christopher explained. "But you can't, though, Nana."

Ouch! Tina could almost hear her mother's jaw hit the floor.

"A-against a tree?" Mrs. Lawrence's eyes appealed to Tina for help.

"Well, you know how boys sometimes do it at a summer camp." That was lame. Of course her mother wouldn't know how boys "did it" at a camp.

Her father chuckled. "Nana wouldn't know about such things, Christopher." He tousled the boy's hair. "She's never been to a camp. But we fellows know what that's all about, eh?"

"Edward!" his wife reprimanded him severely, but

everyone else laughed.

After Mr. and Mrs. Lawrence had seen the rest of the house, which didn't take long, even including the basement, they were introduced to Mutt. Although it was winter, the dog continued to live outside in his doghouse, but Tina now allowed it to come in to meet the guests.

"Shouldn't we call Hazard so Nana and Papa can meet him, too?" Christopher asked, rubbing Mutt's ears.

"Who is this Hazard?" Mrs. Lawrence asked, not addressing her question to anyone in particular. "Christopher has mentioned him often."

Tina chose to let Christopher do the explaining.

"Nana, I've told you all about him! Don't you remember? He's the chief, and he's Mom's and my best friend. Right Mom?"

Quick, creative thinking had always been Tina's forté. "Yes, he's both our best friend. But we can't have him over now because Hazard is too big to fit in this house while Nana and Papa are here."

Christopher laughed. "No, he's not, Mom! You're joking. We can all fit in here okay."

"Actually I'm not joking. You remember Nana and Papa's house? They're used to having lots of room. This is very different for them."

She'd successfully managed to steer the conversation away from Hazard, as her mother's attention now zeroed back in on the house.

"It certainly is different," Mrs. Lawrence echoed. "But now that it's winter, you must be freezing at night."

"No, we're not," Christopher riposted with a frown,

obviously reacting to his grandmother's negative tone. "This is a warm house."

"Cold linoleum floors," Mrs. Lawrence went on. "Christopher will get sick."

"Nana, I'm not sick." His lower lip stuck out.

"He's never been healthier, Mom," Tina put in. "Not a single cold all fall."

"But there's no room for Christopher to have a desk in his room to do his homework."

Again Christopher hurried to explain. "Mom and I share the kitchen table. She does her teacher-work and I do my homework. It's more fun that way."

Tina was pleasantly surprised by the way Christopher defended his home. She could stop feeling guilty about having brought him here, because it was obvious he loved their little house. How come she'd never realized that? And all the flaws her mother saw were now endearing features also in Tina's own eyes. When had she grown so fond of this little clapboard house?

"How about we walk over to Harold's Diner for a celebratory dinner?" she suggested, putting a firm end to any more negative comments about their home. "It's too late to start preparing a meal."

Mr. Lawrence clapped a fist into his palm. "Great idea. Walking will do us good after sitting all day. Taxi and plane and bus and car. I'm stiff as a board."

Christopher jumped around his grandparents in excitement. "You'll be able to taste Anna's pie. It's the best. And maybe Hazard's gonna be there and you can meet him, too."

"I think Hazard has probably eaten already," Tina said, crossing her fingers. She absolutely didn't want to run into him. They hadn't met since the school

Christmas concert, and she had no idea how he would react when they would meet. Although she knew what she had said was true, she regretted the falling-out her words had again caused between them.

Digging out warm winter clothes from the suitcases and getting dressed took some time, but at last the visitors were suitably bundled up to meet the bitter cold of the December evening.

The snow squeaked under their feet and a million starts twinkled in the clear, black sky as they made their way toward the diner.

All at once Mr. Lawrence pointed up toward the east and exclaimed, "Look! That's Northern Lights over there!"

"Yes," Tina said. "We see them quite often. Aren't they beautiful?"

The luminescent green and pink lights danced on the horizon, at times flaring up to the zenith.

Mrs. Lawrence held onto her husband's arm as she craned her neck to take it all in. "Lovely," she breathed. "How wonderful that you have them right here in your own backyard, without having to travel thousands of kilometres to see them."

Yes, her mother was right. Tina hadn't really appreciated the fact that she now lived so close to the richness and beauty of the clear northern sky, undimmed by electric pollution.

"They always make me want to dance," Christopher cried and began to bounce and twirl around in the snow in his snowsuit and big snow boots. After a few circles he fell, laughing, into the snow bank.

"That was pretty good, but you're not as graceful as the Northern Lights," Tina said. "They never fall to the ground."

Christopher got up and his grandmother immediately brushed the snow off the back of his snowsuit.

"What if they did fall to the ground? Wouldn't that be fun?" she asked.

"Yeah! I'd dance with them and play with them and give them nice names."

"Such as what?" Mrs. Lawrence wanted to know.

"Like 'Glowworm'. Or maybe 'Dancing Bear'."

Mrs. Lawrence laughed. "Very masculine names. I would give them more ephemeral names."

"Like 'Lace Curtains'?" Christopher grimaced and stuck out his tongue.

It didn't surprise Tina that her mother joined in this imaginative activity. Mom had always been playful like that with Christopher, which was the reason his vocabulary included words like "ephemeral". How many other six-year-olds knew what that meant?

They walked on along the snowy road, coming up with names for the Northern Lights. For the time being Tina allowed herself to enjoy her parents' company. Before the visit was over she was sure there would be many moments when she and her mother would clash, and she would end up tearing her hair out. But that was just their natural mother-daughter relationship.

At Harold's Diner most of the tables were full. Christopher looked around for Hazard and Tina knew he was disappointed not to see his friend. She, on the other hand, sighed with relief.

Anna came personally to seat them in a booth, and handed them menus as Tina introduced her parents.

"I'm so glad to meet youse at last. Christopher has told me so much about youse both," Anna said, laughing softly.

"Anna always laughs," Christopher explained. "She's nice."

Mr. Lawrence stood up to shake hands. "I'm happy to meet you. Christopher has told us so much about you."

Mrs. Lawrence smiled and nodded, while Anna laughed.

"Anna, we're gonna have some pie for dessert," Christopher announced. "Is there any blueberry left?"

"Sure is, sweetie-pie." And Anna laughed again.

Tina ordered pork chops and mashed potatoes for her father and fried fish for her mother.

As they waited for their meals, she kept a nervous eye on the door. But when the food came, she turned her attention back to her parents.

"Dad, one would think you hadn't had a meal for weeks," she laughed as Mr. Lawrence dug greedily into his meal.

"This is so delicious," he declared between bites. "Best pork chop I've ever had."

In no time at all he was done and patted his belly, sighing with satisfaction. "I think I've died and gone to heaven."

"If you eat like that you soon will," his wife said, disapprovingly. She turned to Tina. "But this fried fish is excellent. Thank you for suggesting it, dear."

"Hazard caught it today through the ice," Christopher told her. He licked his fork and placed it correctly on his plate to signal he was done.

Thank goodness he'd retained some of his table manners, so Tina wouldn't have to hear any negative comments about that from her mother.

But it surprised her that Christopher knew about Hazard's activities. "How do you know he went ice fishing today?" she asked.

"He told me."

"He told you?" Tina dabbed her mouth with her napkin. "But you haven't seen him since the Christmas concert."

"I called him this morning to tell him we were going to pick up Nana and Papa."

Tina was jolted by the revelation. "I didn't know you two were into calling each other."

"I just call him sometimes."

Mr. Lawrence got into the conversation. "Now who exactly is this Hazard whom Christopher is allowed to call whenever? The boy is too young to be calling just anybody."

"Oh, but Hazard's not just anybody," Christopher reassured his Papa. "I told you, he's the chief. And he's Mom's best friend."

Her mother's questioning eyebrow told Tina this issue would be fully discussed and dissected at a later time.

But just then Anna came to clear up the dishes and hand out the dessert menus. "You wanted pie, right?"

And as Mrs. Lawrence tasted the first forkful of the flaky crust of Anna's blueberry pie, she looked like she had entered the same culinary heaven as her husband had, earlier.

"Ahh," she sighed. "I have never had anything that comes close to this. It is absolutely the best pie crust I have ever tasted. And the filling is simply delicious."

"The blueberries were picked from the forest nearby. Anna has them in her freezer," Tina said and relief washed over her. Hazard hadn't come. She'd dodged the bullet one more time.

Or so she thought.

Hazard walked in through the door. With his hand he brushed the snow off his black hair, leaving it damp and glistening. Tina had to swallow. He looked devastatingly handsome in his black bomber jacket, with a five-o-clock shadow darkening his strong chin. When he smiled at a friend in one of the booths, his eyes crinkled, and Tina heard her mother gasp.

"Who is that good-looking young man?" Mrs. Lawrence whispered, looking as star-struck as a teenager at a rock concert. "He should be in the movies."

Tina wanted to duck behind her menu, but Christopher had turned and already had seen Hazard. Luckily he was sitting in the booth beside his grandfather and couldn't scamper out, but there was no way he could be stopped from calling out.

"Hazard! Hey, Hazard! Come here and meet my Nana and Papa."

Hazard looked up and Tina saw his eyes flash when he saw her. As he leisurely strode over, she wanted to slide under the table, but she had to sit there, pretending she was delighted to see him, while Christopher made the introductions.

Mr. Lawrence stood up to shake hands with Hazard, while his awestruck wife only stared mutely up at him. Under different circumstances Tina would have found this hilarious, but tonight her emotions were in too much turmoil for her to laugh.

"Hi, Hazard," she said. "You've come for a nightcap?" Luckily there was no room in the booth for a fifth person, so she couldn't invite him to join them.

"Just walked over for a beer." His eyes passed over her quickly and didn't linger.

"Is it snowing out there?" Mr. Lawrence asked. "Did you see the Northern Lights?"

Hazard nodded. "I did, earlier, before it clouded over and began to snow." He raised a hand to signal his departure. "Well, it's a pleasure to meet you. I'm sure we'll see you again while you're here."

But Mr. Lawrence wasn't done. He still stood facing Hazard. "Christopher said you went ice fishing today. Do you go often?"

"Most days for an hour or so." Hazard rubbed the back of his neck looking uneasy.

Her father's next question came out of the blue and left Tina staring at him flabbergasted.

"If I may be so bold, I would like to come along sometime."

Now it was Hazard's turn to look surprised. "Sure, of course. Just call me when you want to go and we'll arrange it. Nice to have met you both." He nodded at Mrs. Lawrence, gave Christopher a thumbs-up sign, and left.

Without a word to Tina. Or even a glance.

Mr. Lawrence sat down again. "Nice young man."

Mrs. Lawrence still looked stunned, like she'd dropped out of a tree on her head. "What a handsome young man," she repeated, sounding almost breathless. "Did you say he was your friend?"

"He's the chief. He's Mom's BFF," Christopher piped up.

Tina wanted to kick him under the table.

Mrs. Lawrence looked puzzled. "BFF?"

Christopher sighed impatiently. "Best friend forever.

Geesh, Nana, don't you know anything?"

After Mr. Lawrence had paid for their meals, they walked home in the gently falling snow. It was a beautiful ending to a day that had turned out much better than Tina had expected. Except that Hazard wasn't speaking to her.

Guilt and relief tore at her.

Hazard removed his snowy boots in the small porch before entering Anna's living room. "Merry Christmas," he said to Harold and George, who were watching TV with cans of beer in their hands. Hazard removed his jacket and heaped it on top of the coats already piled up on the wall-hooks of the entry. "That turkey smells damn good."

"Merry Christmas, Chief," Harold said with a wave of his beer can. "Grab a cold one and place your ass on a cushion."

Anna came from the kitchen, wiping her hands on her apron. "Merry Christmas, Hazard." She laughed softly and handed him a can of beer, already unzipped.

"Thanks." Hazard threw himself into one of the armchairs and took a gulp. "What's on the tube?"

"Some old Christmas movie," George said. "It's the one they show every year, with the old guy and the ghosts that visit him."

"Christmas Carol?"

"Yeah."

Hazard knew all about ghosts. Ghost of Christmases past, before he knew Tina. Ghost of Christmas present when wanted to be with her, but couldn't. And—most painful of all—Ghost of Christmas yet to come when she wouldn't be here any more. Once more the fist hit him painfully in the chest. Could there be a more appropriate movie for him to watch?

But Harold flicked it off and relaxed back for a chat. "Got enough wood for the winter? Gonna be a cold one, they say."

"Yeah, I think I'm okay."

"George, here's been sawing and splitting all fall so we're fixed pretty good, too." His words were slightly slurred and his watery eyes shone. Obviously he had already started celebrating the holiday earlier in the day.

"Got anything planned for the New Year?" Harold wanted to know next.

"You mean like whooping it up on New Year's Eve? Or plans for next year?"

"Next year. Thinkin' 'bout them roads 'round here come spring. Damn near jars the teeth outa me— whatever I got left—when I drive on 'em. You thinkin' of gettin' 'em fixed?"

Where had he heard that before? Tina had commented about the pot holes the first day she came here. Had he done anything about them? No. Instead he had brushed her off as a pesky intruder.

"We'll be discussing getting the roads planed in the spring. And adding some gravel on them. Right now you can't complain because the snow's made the roads nice and smooth. Right?"

Harold burped. "Yeah. But when the thaw comes, they're gonna be one big muddy pot hole. Last spring damn near swallowed up my truck."

Hazard took another gulp of his beer. "I don't think they're ever that bad."

"You ain't been 'round here for a few years, son."

Harold pointed at Hazard with his beer can. "You came home last spring after the roads had dried some. 'Member?"

Harold had a point there. "Guess you're right. I'll make sure they're looked after this coming spring."

What else should he be looking after? He'd better start getting busy, before Tina or Harold or someone else pointed out more deficiencies at the rez. Although it didn't take much pointing to see a whole whack of problems, from drafty houses to just plain lack of jobs. Lots of things needed to be done and it was up to him to get things moving. But at least the school had good toilets and nice new linoleum floors. Thanks to Tina's persistence. Just needed another teacher. Maybe even two.

"Okay, everyone," Anna called from the kitchen. "Everything's on the table. Come and dig in. Gobble, gobble." She laughed at her own joke.

And though Anna's food was delicious, Hazard's brain was now in overdrive, thinking of all the things that, come spring, he should be looking after at Greenstone.

Chapter Twelve

Tina had to pinch herself to make sure she wasn't dreaming. Her parents both loved it here at Greenstone!

Hazard had taken Mr. Lawrence ice fishing several times and taught him to fillet the fish he caught. Anna fried them, and once or twice they'd had dinner at Anna's house with more than a few bottles of the fine wine the Lawrences had brought with them. Another time Hazard had invited them to his house where he barbequed moose steaks, which they ate with more fine wine. And when they had a free evening, they enjoyed pork chops and mashed potatoes at Harold's Diner followed by Anna's pie. It was a veritable cornucopia of delicacies for the Lawrences, and Tina couldn't believe how both of her parents sang the praises of the food at the rez.

Mrs. Lawrence asked Anna for the pie crust recipe and spent a morning at Anna's house practicing the art of pie making. She told Tina she wanted to be sure she had it right when she returned to Toronto because she was planning to introduce it to her friends. And whenever anyone mentioned Hazard, she called him the best-looking young man she had ever set her eyes on, including anyone in Hollywood.

At night whenever the Northern Lights danced in the sky, Mr. and Mrs. Lawrence stood outside on the steps, bundled up against the chill, taking pictures to show their friends back home. Or they went for walks to admire the black and endless starry sky.

Who would have believed it? Certainly it wasn't something Tina had ever expected to see, not in her wildest dreams. About the only things her mother couldn't come to terms with was the single bathroom. And the double bed. And Christopher sleeping in the living room on the couch.

Mrs. Lawrence was drying her hair in the kitchen with a big, soft towel—one of the several she'd brought with her and would leave with Tina. She had just had her morning shower, and now her husband slipped into the bathroom, after waiting patiently in the bedroom.

Tina sipped her coffee. "As soon as you and Dad leave, Christopher will be back in his own room and there'll be just the two of us sharing the bathroom," Tina said. "We manage quite well, you know, and using the kitchen sink to brush our teeth in a pinch works very well."

Mrs. Lawrence headed for the bedroom which her husband had just vacated. "Of course it works," she said. "But I still find it quite unorthodox. And speaking of unorthodox things, what exactly is the relationship between you and Hazard?"

Tina blanched. "What's unorthodox about it?" she asked as casually as she could. "He's a friend. Period. End of story." She had to play for time. "Why do you ask?"

"Because to me it looks like . . . how should I put it? Like you are trying to make him keep his distance." She closed the door of the bedroom behind her.

"Is that what it looks like to you?" Tina spoke through the door. The truth, of course, was exactly the opposite. But if she told her mother how much she missed Hazard, it would lead to a discussion about things she didn't want to face.

"Yes, it does," Mrs. Lawrence called from inside the bedroom. "And I don't understand, because he's such a nice young man. I don't mean only nice-looking—which he certainly is, especially when he smiles and crinkles his eyes—but he also has a very wonderful personality, from what I've seen. Christopher seems to like him very much. In fact, I'd say Hazard almost seems like a father to him. And besides that, he is helpful and—"

"Yes, helpful he certainly is," Tina interrupted.

"Why do you sound so sarcastic when you say that?"

Tina was grateful this conversation took place while Mrs. Lawrence was getting dressed in the bedroom. She didn't want to have to face her mother's probing eyes.

"I guess we've had a few issues."

But obviously this vague reply only fanned her mother's curiosity. "What kind of issues? You're not in love with him, are you?"

"No!" Tina yelped. "Of course I'm not in love with him. I mean, if I were, would I be keeping away from him?"

"Yes, possibly you might." Mrs. Lawrence opened

the bedroom door and came out, dressed stylishly, as usual.

"Mom you always look so chic. Where did you buy that outfit?" Tina asked, hoping to distract her mother.

No such luck. Mrs. Lawrence seemed hell-bent on getting to the bottom of this Hazard-issue. She went into the kitchen and Tina had to follow.

"I can't remember where I bought it." She sat down at the table and motioned for Tina to join her. "Before we leave for home, I would like to know what your plans are. I assume you're staying to the end of the school year?"

"Yes. I'm thinking I probably will. The kids need me." And Charlotte, especially, needed her.

"And after that?"

Tina sat down opposite her mother. Explaining things was going to be difficult because although she had made up her mind to stay till the end of June, the situation with Hazard was far from clear. "After that" was a place she tried her best to avoid because she had no idea what she would do.

She'd always assumed she would simply go back to Toronto and move into her new condo, but as the golden northern autumn had turned to winter, that idea seemed less and less enticing. She and Christopher liked it here at Greenstone. They were happy living in their little house and their neighbours were friendly.

And after the successful Christmas concert, she was feeling very positive about teaching, even if no replacement for the bigger kids was forthcoming for the spring term. She'd decided a one-room schoolhouse wasn't such a bad thing, especially with all the improvements to the portable, as well as the new composting toilets. Yes, the kids still had to run outside, but the new outhouse was heated, with ceiling lights, and walls that were painted a sunny, warm yellow.

Charlotte's situation still was worrisome, but Tina hoped to come up with a solution if she thought long and hard about it. A solution that wouldn't involve her becoming a mother to a newborn baby. Surely some other answer would surface. From somewhere.

But the problem between her and Hazard seemed insurmountable. Somehow they could never go for any length of time without clashing. And as for staying here . . .

While Tina sat, deep in thought, Mrs. Lawrence poured coffee for them both.

"And after that?" she asked again.

"I don't know, Mom," Tina conceded sadly. "I wish I knew, but—"

"Does he love you?"

The question made Tina's hand jerk and she spilled coffee on the arborite table.

It seemed her mother took that as a "yes", because she continued. "So he has said he loves you. What did you say to him?"

Tina's chair scraped back as she jumped up. "Mother!" she cried in desperation. "I don't belong here."

"Why not?" Mrs. Lawrence calmly went to put two slices of whole wheat bread into the toaster and took out a jar of blueberry jam from the fridge. "It says here this jam was made by someone called Tracy. Does she live on the reserve?"

"Yes. She picks blueberries and makes jam at home. It's very delicious." Tina hoped this would distract her mother from the subject they were discussing.

Mrs. Lawrence dipped the tip of a knife into the jar and tasted. "Yes, it certainly is. Almost as delicious as Anna's pie. But why do you say you don't belong here, dear?"

Tina sighed. Obviously there was no way of distracting her mother when she was on a hunt for answers.

Why didn't she belong here? Not because she didn't like the people of Greenstone or her students. Not because she didn't love her little home. Not because she didn't find the sparkling lake and the nature around her peaceful and beautiful.

It was because of Hazard she didn't belong here. They didn't see eye to eye on anything and were always butting heads. The only thing that united them was sex and, wonderful as it was, that was not enough for her.

But what about love? Hazard had told her he loved her, but as long as the future was still undecided, she didn't want to tell him what was in her heart. Yes, she loved him. And yes, she wanted to be with him. She wanted to live here in Greenstone and be his wife. But for that to work, they needed some common ground to build on. It was not in her nature to sit back and simply watch, passive and uninvolved. But Hazard saw her only as a meddling do-gooder, looking down her nose at his people.

She wanted to be a part of whatever he was planning for the good of the town. She wanted to be there beside him, working with him. And she also had many ideas she wanted to share with him. Maybe some of them were just pie-in-the-sky schemes, but she didn't want them to be shot down without discussion as the ramblings of a meddling busy-body.

Tina sighed again. No, it wasn't going to work.

"Hazard thinks I am too opinionated," Tina finally conceded aloud. "Every time I suggest something, he takes it as though I'm criticizing his people. But I'm not. I'm just bringing up ideas to improve their life. Is that so wrong?"

"Maybe their lives don't need improving. I know you want to help make things better, but sometimes people's lives are fine just the way they are."

"But the young people have no jobs!" Tina cried. "All they do is hang around Harold's Diner. They go fishing or hunting sometimes, which is all good, but . . . "

"What do you think they should do instead?" Mrs. Lawrence buttered the toast and handed a slice to Tina. She dipped the knife into the jam and spread the preserve on her bread. "I think it's so cute that Christopher bakes bread. My little grandson, the baker!" She bit into her toast and jam. "It's very nice and crunchy toasted. I love it. So what do you think the young people should do instead?"

Geesh! Mom wasn't giving up! Tina played for time by chewing her toast very thoroughly and then taking a sip of coffee. Should she share her ideas with her mother? She had never even told Hazard about them because he would feel she was meddling in the reserve affairs.

"Well, since you ask . . ." she at last began. "I've been thinking about the fact that there are so many opportunities here for an eco-tourism business. I heard about it some time ago, and since then have been reading up on it on the internet and thinking about it non-stop. It seems to be the in-thing these days, you know. People want to experience something different when they go on their holidays, something that would teach them about the First Nations people in Canada. It's happening all over the world, you know. In USA, in Australia, in New Zealand, and even in countries where the Sami live, like Norway and Finland. People want to learn about the culture and heritage of people who've been around for thousands of years, but whose ancient ways have almost been forgotten. It's a win-win situation. It would give jobs to people on the rez and they could proudly show off their culture and heritage to interested tourists.

"We have these beautiful pristine lakes around here, and forests with moose and deer. People already like to come here to hunt and fish. If we built wilderness camps they could rent, that would bring in money. And the young people could act as guides and help these fishermen with their catch, the way Hazard helps Daddy with the cleaning and filleting. Do you see where this could lead?" Tina was getting more and more excited as she talked.

Her mother smiled and put down her empty coffee cup. "This is so like you, Tina." She patted Tina's hand on the table. "It reminds me of the way you used to get all excited when you were young, and thought of some brilliant idea to help the less fortunate. Some of them weren't very practical, of course, but to me these ideas of yours are very sound."

Tina let out a breath of relief. "Thank you, Mom."

"And you haven't told Hazard about any of this?"

"Heavens, no!" Obviously Mom didn't have a clue about these proud leaders. "He would think I'm butting my nose into reserve business. He's really prickly about me saying anything about his people. He would say it sounds like I think the people are lazy and stupid since they haven't already thought of it or done it."

"Oh?"

"Yes, and he would accuse me of trying to be a Mrs. Fix-it or a do-gooder." She pointed her coffee cup at her mother. "And don't you go saying anything to him, Mom!" Tina cried. "I know how you like to stick your nose into other people's business. You're always trying to give ideas to your help regarding their private affairs."

Mrs. Lawrence frowned. "Only if I have something to say that is helpful."

"Something *you* think is helpful."

"It usually is," Mrs. Lawrence said decidedly and took a sip of her coffee.

"Now I know where I get my 'helpful' nature from," Tina put air quotes around the word. "From my 'helpful' Mom." Air quotes again.

"Stop with the sarcasm, dear." Mrs. Lawrence got up to clear the plates off the table.

"But now what?" Tina also got up and ran hot water into the sink.'

"You need a dishwasher, Tina. No woman should be without a dishwasher."

"I don't need a dishwasher, Mom. When there's only Christopher and me we do the dishes together. It's a good skill for him to learn."

"Definitely, if you plan to stay here."

Tina's jaw dropped. She turned from the sink to look at her mother, who didn't even sound dejected when she said this. Not upset at the idea of her daughter and grandson staying at Greenstone! What was going on?

"What exactly are you saying, Mom?"

"Come and sit here for a minute, Tina. Bring those cups back and heat up that leftover coffee. And hand me one of those cookies that Christopher made with Anna. They are so delicious. I wish I could take Anna back with us to Toronto to be our cook."

What was she hearing? Tina dried her hands on a terry towel and sat down after refilling their cups. With a start she remembered what she had said to Hazard about this very thing. Those words had caused their latest conflict.

"Mom? Are you feeling okay?"

Mrs. Lawrence put a hand on Tina's arm. "Tina, I'm not blind. And I wasn't born yesterday. No grandmother who loves her grandson could fail to rejoice in how healthy Christopher looks. He's so rosy-cheeked and I can still see some colour on his arms from last summer. He must have been quite tanned."

"Um . . ."

"And his legs look so much stronger than when he left home. He seems always to be running, doing something with James and Chogan. And with that dog of his. That Mutt."

"Um . . ."

"He's so independent," Mrs. Lawrence went on, while Tina simply sat, stunned into silence. "I don't recall him once asking me for help with anything. At

home I used to always have to help him with every little thing."

"I thought you liked helping him," Tina at last was
able to speak. "I thought it made you feel needed. You
never indicated you resented it."

"Oh, goodness, I didn't resent it!" Mrs. Lawrence
cried. "Of course not. And yes, it made me feel needed.
But I also knew it wasn't making him into an independent boy. Your father sometimes scolded me for
helping him, but you know how small he was, so help-
less . . ." Her voice trailed off.

"That's when he was a baby," Tina said. "And he
would have remained a baby as long as you—I guess
we both—kept him a baby. But I didn't know Daddy
was against that. I thought he was on your side."

"No, he was not. He believes in personal independence. He's the one who wanted you to go to camp every
summer so you would learn to do things on your own
and become independent. I admit I wanted to keep you
close to home, so you wouldn't get hurt or stray too
far. And not get in trouble."

Tina laughed. "I did become independent, and I did
get in trouble, and had to move back home with my
baby. I guess I always resented living at home again
like a little girl after being on my own for so long, but
I felt it was better for Christopher when he was little.
And then I took the plunge and moved here."

"To get a way from us."

Somehow her mother's words sounded more like a
confirmation than an accusation, but still it made Tina
feel guilty. "So you knew. But that doesn't mean I don't
love you, because I do love you and Daddy. So very
much." She got up and from behind hugged her

mother around the shoulders. "I just wanted to prove to myself that I was okay by myself, with Christopher."

"And are you?"

"Well . . ." Was she? With Hazard there to help her out, had she really had a chance to prove anything to herself? "I don't know," she at last conceded and sat down again. "I think most of the time I'm okay. And I feel I'm doing a good job with the teaching, but . . ."

"But . . .?"

Tina wished her mother would stop probing. If she told about how she resented Hazard's help, it would sound like she was ungrateful for everything he had done for her and Christopher. But she wasn't ungrateful. Not about everything. Just those things that made Christopher look up to Hazard rather than to her, usurping her role as the authority in his life.

How totally silly that would sound to her mother. Here she was in a new, unfamiliar environment, and she resented the help that was offered to her by someone who knew the ropes. It even sounded silly to her. What had she been thinking? She'd been too proud to accept his help which had been offered in all sincerity. He had never in any way indicated she was ignorant or weak. Never. He had offered his help because that was the kind of a man he was.

And because he loved her.

"Tina, he's a very fine young man, and you could do worse than marry him," Mrs. Lawrence concluded as she took her cup to the sink and washed it out. She picked up the dish towel. "And it's easy to see Christopher loves him, too." She dried the cup and placed it in the cupboard.

Tina's cheeks flashed hot. "Mother, he has not even

asked me," she stammered, flustered beyond belief. "And I doubt very much he ever will."

"Does he know you would stay if he asked you?"

"But I haven't even decided—"

"You would be foolish not to."

Wha-at? Tina couldn't believe her ears. Her mother was encouraging her to marry Hazard? A First Nations man? A non-WASP?

"But, Mom, he's—"

"He's eye candy!"

Tina exploded into laughter. "Mom! What a thing for you to say!"

But Mrs. Lawrence was unperturbed. "Dear, I may be over sixty, but I'm not dead. Nor blind. He's as handsome a man as I've ever laid my eyes on. But more importantly, he is kind and gentle with Christopher, and very helpful and considerate with Daddy. And I understand he is a university graduate with a business degree. That must be useful for a chief to have. What more could I wish for my daughter and grandson? Or for a son-in-law for Daddy and me?" She laughed like a mischievous little girl. "Can you imagine how jealous my friends will be when they see my son-in-law? None of those fuddy-duddies they have as sons-in-law will ever measure up to Hazard."

Tina had to laugh. "Mom, you are so totally incurable!"

"No, just a woman who recognizes a good thing when she sees it." She sat down again and took Tina's hand in both of hers.

This was all coming totally from the left field. "But—but I didn't think you'd want us to live so far away from you," Tina stammered.

"Darling, it's not that far," Mrs. Lawrence said calmly. "Daddy and I have been discussing it and we agree that it will be fun to come and visit you. Daddy loves fishing. Especially ice fishing. And he is already looking forward to our next visit."

Tina's eyes grew bigger and bigger as her mother went on and she struggled to keep her jaw from dropping.

"We can fly here from Toronto in a couple of hours. Of course there's all that tiresome waiting and lining up, but we're retired and have oodles of time. And you can come and visit us during your summer breaks, and when Christopher is older, he can fly down to visit us on his own."

"Mother! Are you telling me you and Daddy have actually been talking about this, as though I were staying here? Like forever?"

"Well, when people get married one hopes it will be forever. But it's not as if you can't come to Toronto whenever you wish. Our door is always open. We can call the realtor when we get home and put your condo up for sale, if you wish. Then, when you move in with Hazard, Daddy and I can stay here, in this cute little house, just the two of us. We can put an addition on it for a second bathroom and a bigger bedroom that holds a king size bed." Mrs. Lawrence clasped her hands together against her ample bosom. "The two bedrooms can be for visitors. Oh, it will be such fun! A little summer cottage."

"But—but I haven't even said I love him," Tina again stammered. This was so totally unreal that she wondered if she was even awake. Maybe she was just dreaming it all.

"Not to him, maybe, but your eyes have said it to me. I'm your mother, remember?"

Tina got up and walked over to the window and stared out to where the morning was breaking and promising a sunny but very cold day.

Yes, she did love Hazard, but she also knew the relationship just wasn't going to work.

Chapter Thirteen

A few days after Christmas Tina and Christopher drove the visitors back to Spruce Falls to catch a bus for Big Thunder. It still was difficult for Tina to digest all her mother had said. How could her impression of her mother have been so wrong? Mom wasn't as narrow-minded as Tina had, for most of her adult life, believed her to be. She was a strong-minded woman, yes, but seemed to be open to new ideas and ready to accept changing conditions. And, most surprising of all, she didn't look down her nose at the residents of Greenstone. Well, not all of them, anyway. She thought highly of Anna and couldn't stop admiring the skills of Harold, who had presented her with a pair of his softest moccasins, decorated with Susan's fine beadwork. It almost made up for his overindulgence of alcohol, although Mrs. Lawrence couldn't stop herself from trying to educate him on the health benefits of temperance.

And she never stopped telling Tina how impressed she was with Hazard's considerate manners toward her, and with his kindness and helpfulness toward her husband, who loved to be taken fishing whenever

Hazard had a free moment. And she couldn't say enough about the warm relationship he had with Christopher. In fact she often commented on how her grandson considered Hazard to be part of the family. And every day she gave not-so-subtle hints about his desirability as her son-in-law.

Now, as they drove toward Spruce Falls, Mrs. Lawrence once again broached that very subject. "I expect you to keep me posted on the situation between you and Hazard," she said to Tina. She sat in the front, while Mr. Lawrence and Christopher were engrossed in some loud guessing game in the back seat.

"There's nothing to post," Tina said impatiently.

"There will be," her mother said firmly. "He's not the kind of man who lets important matters like this slide by him. You indicated he has said he loves you."

Tina's heart took a huge leap, sending blood up to her cheeks. "But I'm sure he just said it in the heat of the moment and didn't really mean it, Mom," she said as defiantly as she could. The effect was almost spoiled by her voice that refused to remain steady.

"I'm sure he meant it. He is not the kind of man who speaks idly of such important matters." And having thus made her pronouncement Mrs. Lawrence turned to look at the scenery, signaling the matter was now closed. It also implied she considered herself to be correct.

Tina remained silent. She didn't want to part with her mother on a quarrelsome note because it would be over half a year before they would see each other again. They had talked of Tina and Christopher flying to Toronto in July, after school was out, but Tina hadn't made it clear if it would be for a visit or a permanent stay.

Heck, she didn't even know herself what the situation would be at that point in time. Would she continue to teach in September or call it quits? She had told her parents not to put her condo on the market until she was absolutely sure.

After her parents had boarded the bus, and all the final waving was done, Tina and Christopher headed back to Greenstone. The car felt strangely empty and even Christopher noticed the difference.

"Is this car too big for just us?" he asked.

Tina smiled. "We'll have to invite James and Chogan along more often to fill it up."

But when they entered their little house, he stepped into the living room and, without even removing his outer clothes, spread out his arms and twirled around a few times. Tina couldn't tell it if was from relief, or because the house, also, now felt huge to him.

"It's nice to have our home back again," he said, clarifying the issue. "I don't want any more visitors, even if it's Nana and Grandpa. They take up too much space."

"What about when James and Chogan come to play?" Tina asked. And couldn't help adding," Or Hazard comes to visit."

"James and Chogan don't stay here," Christopher said. "They go home after we finish playing. And Hazard's different."

"How's he different?" She was very curious to hear his view on the man.

"Because he's kind of like a daddy," Christopher explained while removing his blue down jacket—a gift from his grandparents. "Every home should have a daddy. Right, Mom?"

Tina was glad he was busy putting up his jacket in the hall closet, because her face went up in flames and her heart pounded a fierce tattoo. Not Christopher too! Everyone was trying to tell her the same message. Of course Christopher's message wasn't a deliberate one, like her mother's, but still . . .

After swallowing a few times she was able to respond. "Every house does not have a daddy, Christopher. And we've been happy here without one, haven't we?"

"Yeah, but still it's nice when Hazard's here." With that he went to turn on the TV and slouched down on the couch. After a while, to Tina's chagrin, he continued. "Couldn't we ask him if he'd like to be our daddy?"

Tina stopped on her way to the kitchen to prepare dinner. What could one say to that? The plain truth, of course.

She turned back and came into the living room. "A man doesn't just decide to become a daddy, Christopher. It's something a man and a woman decide together."

"So why don't you and he decide it together?"

The innocent question required a complicated answer. Tina took a few deep breaths and then made a stab at a reply. "The man and woman must first decide that they love each other and want to live together forever. Then he can become a daddy."

"Well, I know you love Hazard, because you're always happy when he's around. And he loves you."

Tina's hand flew to her breast. Had Hazard said something to the boy? "How do you know that?"

Christopher turned to look at her. His big, blue

eyes beamed into her with innocence. "Because I saw you guys kissing once. Remember? You told me people kiss when they love each other. Right?

Oh God! Had Christopher seen them? "When did we kiss?" she coughed out.

"Remember when he was leaving that one time and you were kissing him good night?"

She sighed with relief. He'd not witnessed anything more passionate. "Oh, yes, that time. I was kissing him good night, just like I kiss you good night."

"You kiss me because you love me, and so you kissed Hazard because you love him. Right?" Christopher seemed totally comfortable with his logic. And Tina couldn't argue with it, either.

"Right," she whispered, and turned to go into the kitchen.

It was New Year's Eve. Tina and Christopher had just Skyped Toronto and wished her parents Happy New Year before Mr. and Mrs. Lawrence left for the Gala dinner-dance at their Country Club. Mr. Lawrence had been in a jubilant mood, looking forward to bragging to his friends about going ice fishing with Hazard and the catches he'd made. But it was Mrs. Lawrence who again upset Tina's equilibrium.

"I'm going to tell my friends about the handsome and well-educated First Nations Chief who, I hope, will soon be my son-in-law."

Luckily there was no time to get into a long discussion as the Lawrences had to leave for the party.

"Don't get your hopes up, Mom," Tina said as she closed the connection. A whole lot of good that did. Her mother had already made up her mind. Never mind that her daughter had no idea what she would do.

Hazard hadn't contacted her since her parents had left. And even before that, they had only spoken to each other when absolutely necessary, just enough so it wouldn't be obvious something was wrong between them.

There was a knock on the door and Tina's heart zoomed to her throat. Hazard.

But it was Florence, and Tina's heart settled back into a normal rhythm.

"Hi, Florence," she called out cheerfully, hiding her disappointment. "Happy New Year!"

"Yes, Happy New Year," Florence responded and shook the snow off her shoulders in the tiny porch. It had been snowing since early evening, covering up the countryside with a clean, white blanket.

"Come in and have a cup of coffee with me," Tina said. "Christopher went to take Mutt for a walk and was going to drop in to wish James and Chogan Happy New Year."

Florence removed her snow boots and then entered. In her shyness she almost hugged the walls as she walked down the hall into the kitchen.

Tina set out coffee mugs and placed a few muffins and cookies on a plate for them. She and Christopher had already had their dinner, and she assumed Florence had also eaten.

After drinking a cup of coffee and eating a cookie, Florence at last unveiled the purpose of her visit. Of course Tina had assumed it wasn't just to wish her Happy New Year.

"I wanted to talk about Charlotte," Florence said.

Tina frowned, taken totally off guard. "Charlotte?

What about her?"

"My husband and I have been thinking that we'd like to adopt the baby," Florence explained. "We can't have any more children but we both would like to have a little girl. A sister for James and Chogan. We heard it's going to be a girl."

Tina was elated but tried not to show it. "Well . . ." she began. "Have you spoken with Charlotte about this?" Florence's offer certainly opened up an ideal situation. Charlotte would be able to go to high school in the fall and the baby would be in a good home right on the rez. And Charlotte would be able to see her child whenever she was home."

"Not yet," Florence said. "We wanted to talk to you first since we know Charlotte wanted you to have the baby. We didn't know how you felt about giving her up."

"Yes, well . . . since I'm not at all sure about my plans for the future, this sounds like an ideal offer. I will speak to Charlotte about it, and I'm sure she'll be willing to consider it. Thank you, Florence."

After Florence left, Tina waited for Christopher's thumping at the door but when it didn't come, she picked up the phone.

"I want to stay and play a bit longer. Okay, Mom?" Christopher said. "We're building a big city from the blocks Santa brought them."

"All right. It's getting late but since it's New Year's Eve you can play one more hour. At ten thirty sharp I want you and Mutt to be home."

"Yea!"

Okay, then. She would be alone on New Year's Eve. No problem. There was always something on TV. She went to turn it on, and then poured herself a glass of wine. Her parents had left her a bottle of fine champagne for New Year's Eve, but drinking it by herself just didn't cut it.

She flicked through several channels, looking in vain for something interesting. Watching New Year's celebrations around the globe failed to raise her spirits tonight. She was in no mood to celebrate.

But then the thumping of boots at the door sent a shiver of premonition through her. It wasn't time for Christopher to come home yet. And the thumping was much too loud for his small boots. It was followed by a knock. Definitely not Christopher.

With tremulous steps Tina went to answer.

Hazard swept the snow off his hair with his fingers. Obviously he'd walked here, judging from the snow on his shoulders.

"You should wear a hat," Tina said. Something safe to begin with.

"It's not that cold," he replied. "May I come in?"

"Of course." She managed to get the words out despite the sudden dryness in her mouth.

Hazard brushed the snow off his shoulders before removing his jacket. Then he took off his boots and stepped into the living room on stocking feet.

What was his reason for coming? It couldn't be just a social visit. They hadn't had one of those since before the Christmas concert.

"Sit down, please. What can I get you?" Tina asked. "I just poured myself a glass of wine to celebrate New Year's Eve. Would you like one?"

"Sure. That would be fine." He sat in his customary place on the couch and Tina's heart gave a jolt of pleasure at the familiar sight.

She handed him a glass of red. "So what brings you here?" She wanted him to know she didn't expect this to be a social visit. Though she hoped and prayed it was.

It wasn't.

"I wanted to talk about next September," Hazard said, and Tina's hopes and prayers took a crash dive. "I have to advertise for an intermediate teacher for the spring term, and I thought I might as well advertise for a primary teacher for September at the same time. If you are leaving."

So he was here tonight only in his role as the chief, concerned about the upcoming school year. Which was good. Nothing wrong with that. Except that Tina wished he'd come to see her, personally, and to wish her Happy New Year.

But of course he wouldn't do that, unless he was willing to forgive her for what she had said about the people on the rez. How wrong she had been! Her mother had told her she would have loved to bring Anna to Toronto as her cook, so what Tina had said about these people not being good enough even to be servants in the world of the Lawrences was totally not so.

Hazard sipped his wine silently, waiting for her reply. But what could she say? Yes, she'd already admitted to herself she loved him. And yes, he'd told her he loved her. But how much weight did that carry? Even if they loved each other, there was no hope in the long run for their relationship to succeed if their personalities continued to clash.

If he felt Tina had a low esteem of the Greenstone

residents, why would he even want her to stay as their teacher? He was wrong, of course, because she had grown to appreciate the residents and to love the children, but would he believe her if she apologized? She needed a chance to redeem herself.

"Listen, Hazard," she began tentatively. "I want to let you know something before we talk about whether I should stay or go."

He raised his brows, obviously surprised. "Yeah?" Did she see a glimmer of hope in his eyes?

She took a sip of her wine although she wanted to gulp it all down to give her courage. "Of course you remember what I said at the school Christmas party about the people here not being good enough to be servants in the homes where my parents live."

"Yes." His voice took on a dark, defensive tone and he seemed to close up, right before her eyes.

"Well, I was wrong." She took another sip.

"What do you mean?" He didn't sound any friendlier. Though slightly less defensive, perhaps.

"I was wrong. My mom was ready to shanghai Anna back home with her to be her cook. She didn't care a whit that Anna is Indigenous. She just appreciated that Anna is a great cook and a fabulous baker." Another sip. A big one this time.

"Yeah?" He sounded a bit more receptive.

"Yes. And Mom didn't turn up her nose at everything here at Greenstone like I though she would. She was a bit—I should say quite—shocked about the lack of some conveniences, like just one bathroom, and that they had to sleep in a double bed, but she made do and adjusted much better than I gave her credit for." She paused and reached for the bottle to pour herself more wine.

Hazard was sitting up now, looking at her. "So everything you said at the school Christmas party was based on your own preconceived ideas?"

Tina nodded. "Pretty much. I expected Mom to judge Greenstone with the same yardstick she used at home. I didn't expect her to be so thrilled with the food at Harold's Diner, or to be tolerant of Harold's drinking, or accept that Christopher's hands weren't always clean."

"I see."

"Both Mom and Dad think the sun rises and sets on you. I want you to know that you made quite the impression on them and they're already planning their next visit. Dad might soon show up with a friend or two so I hope you'll be ready to take them fishing." She smiled and Hazard grinned back at her. Seeing his eyes crinkle made the sun come out especially for her on a snowy winter's night.

"Mom thinks you're the greatest thing since the proverbial sliced bread," she added. But no way was she going to tell about her mother wanting him for her son-in-law.

Hazard stood up and held out his hand to her. "Come here, Tina."

But she had to finish saying what she'd started. She stood her ground although every cell in her body wanted to rush into his arms. "Hazard, can you try to forget my haughty words and forgive me? I was wrong to say those things and I'm so sorry."

"Tina, you were only saying what you thought was the truth." His hand was still extended, and now she reached out for it. She felt his heart beat against hers as he took her in his arms and held her tightly.

"I've missed you, Tina," he murmured. "So very much."

"I've missed you, Hazard." Missed his kisses, his loving, being in his arms, talking with him. She'd missed everything about him so much.

And then he kissed her, deeply, hungrily, making her strain against him for more. His mouth ravaged her and couldn't seem to get enough of her.

"Tina," he groaned. "Please stay. Stay forever. I love you, my darling."

"Yes, I want to stay," she whispered. "Because, Hazard, I—"

There was thumping at the door, and a moment later Christopher announced his snowy entrance. "Hi guys!" He proceeded to remove his jacket, hat and boots while Tina tried to pull away from Hazard's embrace.

But he held on, not letting her go. A wicked grin was on his face, as though he'd guessed what Tina was about to say. "So what were you going to tell me?" he asked.

"Later," she whispered.

"Now." He kept her prisoner, gripping her tightly.

"Let me go," she hissed fiercely.

"Never," Hazard said and the fire in his black eyes sent the blood surging to all the secret places in her body.

Christopher entered the room and stopped. A wide smile spread on his face when he saw them embracing. "Was Mom kissing you or something?"

"Yes, as a matter of fact, she was," Hazard replied, and ignored Tina's scowls.

"That's good. Cause Mom told me when she kisses someone it means she loves him. Like when she kisses me. So that means you love Hazard. Right Mom?"

What could she say? Hazard's intense eyes were holding her captive just like his strong arms.

"Right, Mom?" he mimicked Christopher.

Tina sighed in resignation. "Right."

"Say it then," Hazard demanded, turning her face up to look at him. "I want to hear you say it, Tina."

"I love you, Hazard," she whispered in his ear, so only he could hear.

Hazard's lips were on hers in a brief, but powerful kiss, sealing the words between them.

They pulled apart to share the moment with Christopher, who was jumping around them in excitement.

"Now Hazard can be our daddy!" he shouted.

"Your daddy, Christopher," Tina corrected him.

The boy stopped, puzzled. "What about you?"

"I already have a daddy, remember? Hazard can be my husband."

Hazard's brows shot up in mock surprise. "What? Are you proposing to me, Christina Lawrence?"

Tina blushed, but then shrugged in defiance. "Well, if you won't, I guess I have to. One of us has to get the job done."

"I accept," he said. "But, just to follow old traditions, I guess I should be the one to do the proposing." He dropped down on one knee before her. "Will you marry me and stay at Greenstone to be the chief's wise wife?" Then he quickly added, "And the primary teacher."

Tina laughed. "Pretty clever, Chief Abraham. Two

birds with one stone. But yes, I'll accept both proposi-
tions."

"Yea!" Christopher yelled and ran circles around
them.

Later, after the New Year had been brought in with
whoops and kisses and the clinking of champagne
glasses—even a bit for Christopher—Tina and Hazard
sat side by side on the couch. Having refused to be put
to bed, Christopher had fallen asleep on the floor.

"You know what I've been reading about lately?"
Tina asked somewhat tentatively. She wanted to introduce the idea of eco-tourism to Hazard without making
it sound like she was going to organize the whole thing.

"Haven't a clue," he said lazily, playing with a
strand of her hair.

"Have you ever heard of eco-tourism?"

Hazard sat up and Tina stiffened. Would he get
angry with her for bringing up another one of her
"crazy ideas"?

"Of course I have. Funny you should ask, because
that's what we've been discussing lately at the Band
Council meetings."

Tina listened with surprise and pleasure as Hazard
described a scenario, very similar to what she had
been telling her mother not many days ago. When he
finished she gave him a hearty kiss.

"That sounds absolutely wonderful! I'm looking forward to working with you to achieve all that."

Great minds think alike. She smiled to herself as
she melted into his arms.

About Karen Rossi

Karen Rossi (the pen name of Kaarina Brooks) has been a romantic since she was a child. She and her sister had their own "publishing company" and wrote about love-struck princes and princesses.

Today she writes grown-up romances where modern-day "princes and princesses" go through heart-wrenching relationship struggles before reaching their happily ever after.

She now also has a real publishing company, Wisteria Publications. Besides romances, she also publishes kids' books and non-fiction works, such as a cook book.

She lives in Southern Ontario with her husband and kitty-cat, Lilly.

www.wisteriapublications.com
brooks.kaarina@gmail.com